SATOSHI WAGAHARA

ILLUSTRATED BY ■ 029 (ONIKU)

NEW YORK

THE DEVIL IS A PART-TIMER!, Volume 13
SATOSHI WAGAHARA, ILLUSTRATION BY 029 (ONIKU)

Translation by Kevin Gifford
Cover art by 029 (oniku)

This book is a work of fiction. Names, characters, places, and incidents are the product of the author's imagination or are used fictitiously. Any resemblance to actual events, locales, or persons, living or dead, is coincidental.

Yen On
1290 Avenue of the Americas
New York, NY 10104

Visit us at yenpress.com
facebook.com/yenpress
twitter.com/yenpress
yenpress.tumblr.com
instagram.com/yenpress

First Yen On Edition: April 2019

Yen On is an imprint of Yen Press, LLC.
The Yen On name and logo are trademarks of Yen Press, LLC.

The publisher is not responsible for websites (or their content) that are not owned by the publisher.

Library of Congress Cataloging-in-Publication Data
Names: Wagahara, Satoshi. | 029 (Light novel illustrator) illustrator. | Gifford, Kevin, translator.
Title: The devil is a part-timer! / Satoshi Wagahara ; illustration by 029 (oniku) ; translation by Kevin Gifford.
Other titles: Hataraku Maousama!. English
Description: First Yen On edition. | New York, NY : Yen On, 2015–

Identifiers: LCCN 2015028390 |
ISBN 9780316383127 (v. 1 : pbk.) |
ISBN 9780316385015 (v. 2 : pbk.) |
ISBN 9780316385022 (v. 3 : pbk.) |
ISBN 9780316385039 (v. 4 : pbk.) |
ISBN 9780316385046 (v. 5 : pbk.) |
ISBN 9780316385060 (v. 6 : pbk.) |
ISBN 9780316469364 (v. 7 : pbk.) |
ISBN 9780316473910 (v. 8 : pbk.) |
ISBN 9780316474184 (v. 9 : pbk.) |
ISBN 9780316474207 (v. 10 : pbk.) |
ISBN 9780316474238 (v. 11 : pbk.) |
ISBN 9780316474252 (v. 12 : pbk.) |
ISBN 9781975302658 (v. 13 : pbk.)
Subjects: CYAC: Fantasy.
Classification: LCC PZ7.1.W34 Ha 2015 | DDC [Fic]—dc23
LC record available at
http://lccn.loc.gov/2015028390

ISBNs: 978-1-9753-0265-8 (paperback)
978-1-9753-0266-5 (ebook)

1 3 5 7 9 10 8 6 4 2

LSC-C

Printed in the United States of America

PROLOGUE

Just as the cloak of night was being drawn across the twilight sky, *it* had reached the home of a set of human beings, its precarious grip on life resisting the darkness.

Its sharp eyes pierced through the darkness, its growling all but forcing anyone near to focus upon it. Its frame was large, all too large compared to others of its kind. Its stomach was large enough to store vast amounts of prey, and the bright crimson that covered its entire body won over the night itself. It was, perhaps, exactly the appropriate kind of eerie, unseen form to be crawling around at the cusp of darkness.

But there was a simpler way to describe the ominous presence. To be succinct, it was the mount belonging to the Lord of All Demons. The sharpened, glowing eyes; the growl that echoed in your bones; the vast size; the appetite—it was all there so the one at the very peak of demondom would have a mode of transportation befitting his brilliant majesty. And the Lord of All Demons himself was clothed in crimson as vivid as his mount's armor, his determined eyes surveying the human world when darkness began to consume it.

In another moment, the lord and his mount arrived at a human residence, just before the sun abandoned it for good. The poor humans—once again unable to resist the workings of the universe that robbed them of sunlight—had scrambled to project their own light into that darkness, to keep themselves safe by staving off the black that little bit longer.

The crimson-garbed Lord of All Demons left his bright red helmet with his trusty steed as he took an initial merciless step toward the light. His mount closed its glowing eyes, calmed its growling roar, and rested the body that had brought him all this way as it waited. Its master's black feet took step after powerful step forward, edging closer and closer to the mortal domicile.

All that separated him from the inside was a single feeble-looking wooden door. To the Lord of All Demons, it would be child's play to batter it to splinters, but his motivations were elsewhere. For a single moment, he lent an ear to the voices of the humans inside—and then a smile befitting the ruler of the demon realm crossed his face.

He opened his mouth. A voice that made all who heard it look up in anticipation. A voice that stirred the appetites of everyone nearby. A voice that would make anyone open the door for their rightful lord—

"Hello! MgRonald delivery!"

"Oh, wow, it's really you! I'm coming!"

With the young female voice came the sound of a rickety-sounding dead bolt unlocking itself.

"Thanks for coming by!"

"...No worries, Chi."

Sadao Maou, MgRonald crewmember in his standard-issue red Windbreaker, found the tension ease a bit from his salesman's grin, giving Chiho Sasaki a bit more of a sincere smile as he recognized her. He was in front of Room 201 of Villa Rosa Sasazuka, the two-floor wooden apartment building in the Sasazuka neighborhood of Tokyo's Shibuya ward—in other words, his own residence. He himself had walked right through that door this morning, on his way to the MgRonald in front of Hatagaya station, and this *was* well within his restaurant's delivery range. When an order came in, it was the full responsibility of the Lord of All Demons and occasional shift manager Sadao Maou to ferry it over.

But it was with a somewhat cool, nonbusinesslike expression that Maou called to the people inside, removing the combo meals and receipt from his insulated bag and handing them to Chiho.

"Y'know, not for me to say, but honestly, ordering *this* much for two meals in a row is kinda scary."

"Indeed, my apologies. It wasn't my intention earlier this afternoon..."

It was a well-built middle-aged man who replied, his face remorseful.

Meanwhile, Chiho examined the receipt to ensure the order was complete as delivered. "Nord gave everything over the phone that Erone asked him to. I don't know how Acieth found out about it, but she did, and she insisted on throwing some more in, too. Um, this should be all of it."

The man called Nord took a five-thousand-yen bill out of his wallet and presented it to Maou.

"Well, lemme just say, that archangel all you humans are worshipping got fat enough in a week that her BMI's probably up in the next category by now. My job's to deliver whatever you guys order, but you gotta understand, it's the job of a guardian to watch over the health of their kids, y'know? ...Out of five thousand...forty-five yen in change."

"...You have my appreciation." Nord nodded, not having anything to counter with—and just as he did, there was a thumping sound of someone storming up the outside stairs.

"Ooh, that is here!"

"I'm hungry."

"Whoa!"

Two small, thin figures half stumbled into Room 201, zooming right past both sides of Maou. Behind them was a grown woman's voice, chasing upstairs after them.

"Acieth! Erone! Wash your hands before you eat! ...Oh, don't eat straight from the bag like that, you two! At least lay it out on the table first."

"What you want? I am the hungry! Which one did you eat during the lunch, Erone?!"

"This one. It has...um, mayonnaise? I like it."

"Ooh, yes, the mayonnaise is very good! But this I have eaten before. I want the new thing first!"

"The man from this afternoon said that one over there is a seasonal item."

"Ooh, I must eat that! Give it!"

"Okay!"

The two children lunged for their meals—Acieth Alla, a single shock of purple coursing through her silvery hair, and Erone, a single streak of red in his dark locks. The admonishing voice of the grown-up behind them may as well not have existed as they began to eagerly devour the greasy feast before them.

"Wash...your hands, you two..."

The purple-haired woman following behind watched with Nord, a look of exasperation on her face.

"Uh, Laila?"

She awkwardly turned toward Maou, as if just now noticing him.

"You guys are letting Erone and Acieth stomp all over you, aren't you?"

"No, um..."

"Well...I mean..."

"I know Amane and the landlord have their takes on this, and if Chi and Ashiya are okay with it, I don't mind them hanging out in Room 201. But if I come here and there's bits of food and wrapping all over the place, you can't expect the Devil King's Army to take that sitting down, all right?"

""...All right.""

Laila, archangel from heaven, and Nord, father of the Hero of another world, shrugged their shoulders and spoke in tandem at the understandable warning from the fast-food courier.

"Oh, it's all right!" shouted Chiho to quell the heavy atmosphere, both hands balled into fists. "I heard about lunch today, so I brought along some boiled spinach and coleslaw salad I made so Erone and Acieth can have some vegetables!"

Indeed, there were a couple of familiar-looking plastic containers on the table. Maou had seen them many a time.

"Also, Ashiya just went out to buy some fish, since he said eating meat all the time would mess up their diet. He wasn't sure whether to go with salmon or mackerel, though."

"Oh? Well, huh." Maou's face loosened up a bit as he saw Chiho's concern, picturing his faithful retainer and Great Demon General keeping up appearances around the house while he was gone. "Shouldn't you guys be ashamed of yourselves, then? You're grown people. One of you's an angel even."

""We are terribly sorry to have let you down,"" Nord and Laila said, bowing their heads at the Devil King's lecture.

"Ashiya's one thing," Hanzou Urushihara protested in what he knew would be in vain from the side, "but I think you should probably get my permission before Chiho Sasaki's, dude."

He may have been lower on the totem pole than even Chiho, despite being one of the room's permanent residents, but he might have had a point.

"...Well, thank you very much for the order," Maou went on to Chiho, indeed ignoring him. "We look forward to serving you again."

"Thanks, Maou," she replied. "You're closing today, right? Hang in there!"

"Yeah, sorry to make you fill in here for me, Chi. Let Ashiya or Suzuno know before you leave, okay?"

"Sure thing!"

Leaving management of his apartment—his Devil's Castle—to this teenage girl, he hurried down the stairs to Red Dullahan II, his delivery vehicle.

"Devil King! Wait!"

Before he could make it all the way down, a voice from above stopped him. Looking up, he saw his neighbor, Suzuno Kamazuki, leaning over a bit from the landing. A smaller figure was at her legs, eyes open wide and waving in the most darling fashion.

"Daddy! Daddy!"

It was Alas Ramus, Suzuno serving as her nanny while her "parents" Maou and Emi were at work.

"Bye-bye! Hang in dere!"

"...You got it!"

Bottling up his frustration at having to leave her alone, Maou tensed his face and gave an exaggerated wave to his daughter, adding a light nod and stare at Suzuno as a token of his appreciation.

"Right, Alas Ramus. Back inside we go. It's too cold out here."

"Suzu-Sis, c'n I eat Magronato's?"

"I don't know if you can eat as much of it as Acieth can until you grow up a little, Alas Ramus."

"But Accith c'n..."

Maou could barely make out the fading conversation as he

boarded his motorbike and put on his helmet. Getting to hear his daughter's voice helped restore the flagging motivation he had for this shift. Then he heard another familiar voice behind his back.

"Ah, Your Demonic Highness. Keep up the good work."

Maou lifted his visor as he waved at the returning Ashiya. "Yep. You went out to buy some fish?"

"I did—and I tell you, my liege, the incompetence of the Justina family is enough to make me cover my eyes in shame. I see that their children are probing the furthest bounds of gluttony in our landlord's residence as well. Ms. Sasaki and I must teach them the fundamentals of a good diet, or I fear Acieth's and Erone's health will fail them before long."

"Yeah, and if that happens, who knows how the hell that'll turn out, huh?"

Considering the circumstances that led Erone to set up shop in Villa Rosa Sasazuka, Maou figured that maintaining the good health of the children of Sephirah was job number one for all of them. The people closest to these children, though, had next to no interest in putting that into action.

"Sorry to put you through all this."

"Not at all. In the long term, this will benefit our future Devil King's Army. Oh, and would grilled mackerel suffice for dinner tonight, my liege?"

"Sure. Haven't had that in a while."

Maou nodded, undid the side brake on his bike, and fired up the engine.

"See you later for now."

"Very well. Drive safely."

With a wave, Maou set off back to his workplace, making it back without hitting a single red light.

"Oh, perfect. We just got our next order in."

There at MgRonald, as if lying in ambush, was Emi Yusa—Maou's sworn enemy and (of recent days) shift mate behind the counter.

"Here's the address…and here's the order. It'll be ready in three minutes. Kawacchi and Ms. Kisaki are out, so you're up for this one, too, Mr. Maou."

He could never get used to Emi addressing him with a "mister."

"Oh...yeah, this office's ordered with us a bunch of times, haven't they?"

"Right. Ms. Kisaki's handled all the deliveries so far, though. Don't disappoint them."

Emi flashed him a mischievous smile, and he couldn't help but respond in kind. "Don't be stupid."

Mayumi Kisaki, manager of the MgRonald in front of Hatagaya station, had the kind of model-like beauty and proportions that palpably attracted regular customers who'd otherwise go elsewhere.

"I got to see Alas Ramus for a second just now. Looks like she's behaving."

"Yeah, she's never a bother at all when she's at Bell's place. Did my father make that order a moment ago?"

"...Pretty much," Maou said before giving Emi a summary of Nord and Laila's negligent parenting.

"Hmm. I'll have to make up for this with Chiho later..."

"I suppose, but you really need to talk to your parents, you know that?"

"..."

This made Emi pause a bit. Thanks to certain events in the past, relations between her and Laila were about as bad as they had ever been.

"You still haven't really done it, have you? And I don't wanna butt into your family stuff, but it's kind of hurting Chi and the rest of us, so I really wish you could get it over with, y'know?"

"I know, I know..."

As Emi gave the reply—one that indicated she knew all of that but had no interest in translating it into action on her part—Maou spotted a full insulation bag placed on the counter for him.

"Well, back to work. See ya."

"...Sure."

Maou gave a glance at the receipt as he picked up the bag and half jogged out the front door. Soon, the helmet was back on, his butt on the seat, the side brake off, and the key—attached to his belt with a cord—in the ignition. It was now well into the evening as he sped down the city streets, taking the time spent at a red light to think about how depressed Emi looked.

"Well," he mused inside his helmet, "we've been through a lot." And they had. No matter what the circumstances, if you ran into people regularly and started working with them, you couldn't help but start exhibiting all kinds of emotions around them. Smiles and more.

"All part of normal life, I guess."

The light turned green. Maou shook off the cobwebs and twisted the throttle, white vapor coming out from both the tailpipe and his own lips as the city settled itself into winter.

THE DEVIL GETS TOUGH

Off duty this evening and already changed out of her uniform, Chiho returned to the staff room to check whether there were any mistakes on the November shift schedule passed out that day.

Only then did she notice something was off. The schedule was sorted by name first, and Chiho thus knew that she'd always be in row twelve of the spreadsheet. Maou was usually ninth and Emi twenty-fifth, but for whatever reason, Emi was moved up to row twenty-four this month. It wasn't until she began copying her schedule into her notebook that she realized why.

"Oh, right! Kota's gone!"

Kotaro Nakayama, one of the more talented among the younger crewmembers, was the missing row on the sheet.

"He was trying to get a full-time job somewhere, wasn't he? Wow. I guess he really quit."

The thought saddened her just a little as she reexamined the schedule. She had heard the news before—on several occasions, including from Kotaro himself—but seeing his name vanish like this made it seem like time had flown by all too fast.

"No more of him, I suppose..."

Kotaro was a college student, Chiho in high school. One would think their relatively close ages would let them hit it off more, but the two had never engaged in any particularly deep conversation. They weren't enemies, of course, and they talked well enough when they shared a shift. Kotaro, the more experienced of the two, had given her training on more than one occasion even.

But—looking impartially back—apart from the university he went to, the fact he lived somewhere in Hatagaya, and the video games he played as a hobby, Chiho knew nothing about Kotaro Nakayama. She wasn't a gamer at all, so they couldn't talk about that, and when it came to chatting about college life, he was more than likely to do that with fellow student crewmembers Takefumi Kawata and Akiko Ohki.

In more private matters, there was one time when Chiho had mentioned she was on the school team for *kyudo*, the Japanese martial art of archery, and Kotaro replied that his girlfriend practiced Western archery. They then chatted for a while about bow-and-arrow sports—something they kind of but not really had in common. But even that was just ten minutes or so during break, it felt to her.

Really, when it came to veteran part-timer Kotaro Nakayama, Chiho could summarize everything she knew about him in the space of a few minutes. But even so, he was still part of her life, something she treated as a given—and now he was threatening to disappear from memory for good.

It was, to her, quite a surprise. In a way, it felt kind of like when she graduated from middle school. It wasn't like she was besties with the entire student body, but in the space of a single day, the people she always hung out with were gone. It created an unsettling sense of loss.

"What's up, Chi? What're you scowling at?"

"Oh! Ms. Kisaki..."

Mayumi Kisaki, the manager, strolled into the room, removing her hat and earpiece. Chiho looked up at her.

"I was just copying my schedule into my notebook, and I noticed that Kota's shift isn't on here anymore."

"Ah, yeah. I kinda hoped he'd stay on the rest of the year, but even with job interviews and stuff starting later for students than they used to, I guess he really wanted that extra month to balance his course load with all the other prep work he had. That's gonna be a hard hole in the schedule to plug up with new staff, too. It's a big headache."

Kisaki didn't seem too affected by it, but when it came to work, she absolutely never joked or told lies to her staff. Kotaro's absence *did* produce a major hole. With the Hatagaya location in particular, the shift schedule was one thing, but having someone so intimate with all aspects of MgRonald operations depart put that much extra stress on everyone else's shoulders.

"Are you off for today, Ms. Kisaki?" Chiho asked as Kisaki began undoing her tie.

"Nah, there's an emergency regional meeting at another location after this. At this time of the day, no less. Marko's off today, too, so I hope we don't have an emergency here."

She looked at the clock and sighed. Having the main manager out of the restaurant just before the dinner rush made everyone on staff nervous, to say nothing of the other managers not on-site today. With Maou not making any appearance all day, Kisaki honestly wished she could ditch this meeting. In a business like this, having a single person disappear, or not be there, often wound up having much greater impact than at first glance.

"Around the dinner rush, pretty much every location has to deal with personnel shortages…even as our workload keeps going up. If things get any worse, we might have to assign shifts to some of the corporate front office staff." She shrugged. "When it rains, it pours, huh? I got a bunch of other stuff to wrap up, too, so I won't be back today. I'll have my phone on for emergencies, so if anything comes up, just ask Kawacchi or Aki or Saemi, okay?"

"Oh… All right."

Her not being back today struck Chiho in a way Kisaki didn't intend at all. It made the wrinkles around her eyebrows deepen even further. Seeing this, Kisaki (for a change) found it difficult to piece the correct words together.

"Yeah… Though, speaking of, if you think something like that's gonna happen with you, Chi, please let me know sooner than later."

"Huh? What do you mean?"

Chiho didn't quite get her point.

"To be honest, Chi, I really hope you won't fall away from your current schedule, if at all possible—but that's probably not gonna happen, huh?"

"Oh?"

Chiho tilted her head a bit. She never recalled asking for new shifts or extended time off. But it made Kisaki look all the more flustered.

"It's winter of your next-to-last year in high school, isn't it? I bet all your friends are going crazy with college admissions by now."

"College… Ah?!"

She yelped a little louder than she meant, as she finally got Kisaki's gist.

"You're the one in high school, aren't you?" Kisaki smiled a bit, realizing Chiho honestly had no clue. "I don't wanna impose on you simply because you forgot about that, but keep it in mind, all right? It'll be your last year soon, starting in April. I know how much you worry about that kinda thing, so I doubt you aren't treating it seriously. Once you have to start studying for college exams for *real*, that's gonna hurt your shift schedule, right?"

"Y-yeah, I guess it will."

Chiho realized her heart was racing—as if someone had leaped out from around a street corner and yelled, "Boo!" Just the other day, at Emi's friend's place, she had been made to think about the exact same thing—but if the topic shocked her that much this time, then all those ideas of college and exams must have still felt like a distant world to her. Kisaki knew it concerned Chiho greatly, even more than her own family, teachers, or friends knew. It had come up in the middle of her job interview, and Chiho had asked for advice from her manager about the subject several times before.

"Well, when…when the time comes…I'll definitely talk about it with you."

"Great, thank you. It's for your sake as well, after all."

Then, without another word, Kisaki went into the changing room. Hearing her boss close the door behind her, Chiho took a peek at the scene on the dining floor.

"When…I won't be here any longer…"

It hadn't even been a year since she'd begun working here, but sooner or later, she would be leaving the MgRonald family. Chiho didn't know when, but it was definitely coming—and that unavoidable truth felt like a snake coiling itself around her chest. There wasn't any outside air, but it still felt like a cold gust of wind was coming over her. She buttoned up the puffy coat she wore on her way to work and sighed.

"Oh, you're still here?"

"Eeep!"

Chiho leaped into the air at the sensation of someone patting her shoulder from behind.

"Pretty bundled up, huh?"

Kisaki, in her trench coat, gave Chiho a curious look. The teenager hadn't stopped at just her coat—from head to toe, there was hardly a square inch of skin that wasn't covered in several layers.

Chiho meekly explained, "Oh, um, I'm going somewhere else after this, so..."

"Ah. Well, stay warm out there. It's already dark out, so don't stay out too long."

Chiho nodded at the grown-up advice. Kisaki stood next to her, peeking into the restaurant space like Chiho was doing.

"If you don't mind me saying..."

"Yes?"

"I don't think this is someplace you should be intent with staying at forever. It's merely a stepping-stone in your life—for you, for Marko, for Saemi, and for me, too. Everyone needs to find their own place to settle down, you know?"

"...But it hasn't even been a year for me."

Kisaki smiled at the way Chiho assessed her words. "Well, if it seems like just yesterday since you started working here, then I guess you're liking it, huh? But don't be afraid to fret over it. It might seem like you're surrounded by a bunch of older people who've got it all figured out, but they all have the same worries you do, really. Things like, *Did I make the right decision back then?* or *Am I going to make the right call from now on?* and all that."

Hearing this made Chiho realize exactly how obvious it seemed, but until she did, it was difficult for her to even imagine it. She looked at the backs of the MgRonald crewmembers at their stations through the crack in the door and sighed. *Guess everybody's like that. Maybe even Maou and Emi.*

"...Well, I better head off for now."

"Sure thing. Take care."

Either way, this wasn't the sort of problem she could solve by endlessly stewing. Chiho bowed to her manager, briskly put her things inside her bag, and left. The air just outside the automatic doors was crisp against her skin, taking the floor space's warmth away from her cheeks.

"*Am I going to make the right call from now on*—huh...?"

Her sigh melted into the cold air. But she took a decisive step forward anyway.

"Better hurry."

She had to. This was the first day she'd be visiting Room 201 of Villa Rosa Sasazuka as part of Maou and Laila's negotiations.

⁂

One could say the archangel Laila was the original source of the chaos sowed between the two worlds of Earth and Ente Isla—the villain pulling the strings from up above.

As the mother of Emilia Justina, better known as Emi Yusa around here, Laila had finally appeared before Maou and his cohorts. Having known Miki Shiba for the past sixteen years, she was thought to have a great deal of information about Alas Ramus, Acieth Alla, and Erone, the children born from the Sephirah. The two born from the Yesod Sephirah were, by now, indispensable parts of the local residents' lives, and to Maou and Emi, Laila was like a walking, talking font of wisdom that couldn't be more vital to their futures.

To Emi, however, Laila was also a riddle. On one hand, her mother had forced her to slog her way single-handedly through a litany of chaotic disasters; on the other, this woman before her seemed so goofily irresponsible, not at all the evil puppet master she pictured. It made her refuse to deal with her at all—and Maou was the same, his attitude toward her hardening as he attempted to fish information out of her. They had both fought on the front lines up to now, even as Laila lurked around in the shadows, and their discussions had not only failed to bear fruit—they were drifting even further apart than before.

And only a few days after she had appeared in their lives, someone had attacked the subway train Emi and Chiho were riding on, a dark shadow of an attacker totally unfazed by Emi's holy sword and even able to shrug off the powers of Amane Ohguro, child of planet Earth's Sephirah. Laila seemed to know this shade's identity, and as Maou and Emi understood the situation, it was yet another symptom of her machinations. It didn't help relations between them much.

The one thing the demon and half angel agreed on was that neither of them wanted to be dancing to someone else's tune any longer. That applied all the more now that the MgRonald they both worked at began offering delivery service after a long run-up period, making it hard enough just to keep up their regular human being lives.

But they were both half dragged back to the conference table by none other than Miki Shiba and Amane Ohguro. They had captured the shade that had attacked the subway and even gravely injured Laila, reporting to Maou and Emi that the dark fiend was Erone, child of the Sephirah Gevurah paired to Ente Isla. The mystery transformation of his body and Laila's own secrets certainly weren't unrelated, and if they continued to ignore the baggage Laila came to Earth with (as she had put it), there was no telling what would happen to Alas Ramus and her sister Acieth Alla.

Realizing Emi was still reluctant to talk with Laila despite all this, Maou came up with a deal where they would negotiate with the archangel only within the confines of Room 201, with Maou taking Emi's place at the table and accompanied by either Ashiya, Urushihara, Chi, Acieth, or some combination thereof. Laila claimed what happened to Erone wouldn't occur to Alas Ramus or Acieth anytime soon, but between that and the danger to Ente Isla's humanity Shiba had talked about in Urushihara's hospital room, the future facing Maou and Emi seemed dark, foreboding, inscrutable, and ready to pounce upon them at any moment.

*

Chiho had been to Villa Rosa Sasazuka more times than she could count by now, but tonight it seemed like a completely different building to her. It must have been the butterflies at work.

The light in the windows would normally reassure her that she'd be seeing familiar faces soon; now that light seemed oddly cold and indifferent. Normally she'd be able to hear Ashiya and Suzuno and Urushihara yelling at one another by the time she took her first step up the stairway, but today all was quiet. The landing upstairs almost seemed deserted. No sign of Suzuno or Alas Ramus anywhere. It almost made Chiho feel like everyone dear to her had left her in the lurch, as she gingerly pushed the Room 201 doorbell.

"Chi? C'mon in. It's open."

She unconsciously let go of a deep breath. The voice sounded wooden in tone, but it was unmistakably Maou's. The impending (and evidence-free) sense of doom that overcame Chiho made her hang her head a bit, before she recalled the role she was tasked with. Steeling her resolve, she opened the door.

"Hello, it's..."

Then she froze for a few moments.

"...H-hello, Chiho..."

"Hey, Chi. Hope your shift went okay."

"Close the door. It's cold."

The air was chilly. Not metaphorically, either. There was no draft working its way into the apartment, but the ambient air within Room 201 was a good five degrees or so cooler than outside. That much became eminently clear once Chiho caught sight of the three people waiting for her inside.

Maou was wearing a wool cap on his head, the zipper on his UniClo superlight fleece hoodie zipped all the way to the top, and he had two pairs of socks on his feet. The layers covering Urushihara, his back to the front door as he sat by his computer desk, made his shoulders padded and frumpy looking. The collars on each layer of his clothing were haphazardly draped over one another, and even then he had another blanket covering his lap. The only one with a normal-looking outfit was Laila; she wore a dress of somewhat thick fabric but otherwise wasn't shielded from the cold at all. She looked more than a shade paler than before, thanks in part to the way her hair went purple following the subway attack.

The apartment was so chilly that Chiho wondered if that gelatinous block of demonic force they were storing in the closet had sprung a leak. But it wasn't—she felt perfectly fine not having to utilize any of her own holy force to block it. The place was just freezing is all.

"Yeah, see? I told you, when it comes to stuff like this, Chiho never misses a beat. She's always two or three moves ahead of everyone else in the way she preps for stuff. You should learn from her."

"Er...?"

The enigmatic praise from Maou the moment she came in did nothing to cure Chiho's confusion.

"Well," Laila countered, "how was I supposed to expect *this*? Didn't they renovate this apartment several times by now? Why's it even more freezing than outside?!"

It was exactly the question Chiho had, and the tenant had a terse answer for it.

"It's just that kind of building, man."

"...!"

The archangel was forced into silence by the Devil King's frosty declaration.

"Dude, close the door already!" Urushihara called.

"Oh! Sorry!"

Chiho hurriedly did so. It did nothing to warm the room up, but it was still apparently enough to satisfy Urushihara.

"...Did you know about this, Chiho?"

"About...what?"

"About...how cold this place is...?"

"Uhmmm..."

Chiho gave Laila's query a level amount of consideration before remembering the outfit she had on herself: Her favorite earmuffs and scarf. A heavy coat with a sweater under it. Heat-retaining bottoms underneath full-length denim. The low temperature for the day was forecast at around forty degrees, but it'd reached fifty-seven in the afternoon, enough to make her sweat a bit. Right now, though, this wardrobe was perfect for her.

"I...I didn't know exactly, but I knew I was coming here in the evening, so I just kind of naturally went with this."

"Naturally?"

This seemed to amaze Laila.

Maou gave Chiho a satisfied nod. "Yeah, because you know that we don't have any real heating equipment in here. You see? Chi can prep for this kinda thing, I'm sure, because she knows how to pick up on stuff."

"And you're *proud* of that?!" Urushihara and Laila muttered at once.

"You shouldn't let Maou treat that as a badge of honor, Chiho," Urushihara went on, feeling confident enough as a local resident to take Laila's side here.

"Oh, um, I didn't mean to..."

"Well, you are! Thanks to you siding with him, Ashiya's all obsessed with the idea that we don't even need a heater!"

Urushihara took a heavy-looking bag out from beneath his legs.

"This is a hot-water bottle! He says we don't even need to bring out the *kotatsu* table heater until the new year as long as we have this!"

"Um, well, what's so bad about that? I use that when I'm sleeping, too..."

"Yeah, when you're *sleeping*! You ever try cuddling with a hot-water bottle all day at home?!"

"Well, no..."

"Enough, Urushihara," Maou interceded. "Chi isn't wrong. Those things are nice."

"They *ain't* nice, dude! If all the Devil King's Army troops who gave their lives in the invasion of Ente Isla heard you say that, Maou, they'd cry their eyes out until they all became withered husks!"

"Shuddup. We buy an AC or a heater, it's our bank account that's gonna dry up."

"So what's our demonic force *for*, dude?!"

Chiho fully agreed with Urushihara's assertion, but something about seeing him and Maou carry on surprisingly like old times helped ease her initial butterflies. Then, as if timing her change of heart, there was a knock on the door from outside.

"Chiho! Chiho, you are there, I know it!"

"Acieth? Um, Maou..."

"Maou! You may think you hide the smell of Chiho from my nose, but the world, it is not so much easy as that!"

"What is she carrying on about...?"

"We are hungry in the stomachs! If Chiho is there, there must be the fried chicken, too!"

"I...I didn't bring anything this time. I'm just here after work, is all."

"No, Chiho, it's fine," reassured Maou as he rubbed his head, Chiho herself having half withered at Acieth's all-too-sudden appetite. "Nobody would expect you to."

"Oh! Nothing? Aw. Too bad." Surprisingly, it was Urushihara who lodged the first complaint. "Ashiya and Bell have been constricting our diets really badly in order to help Acieth and Erone eat healthier, so I was kinda hoping Chiho Sasaki would have some chicken for us maybe..."

"Wow, Urushihara, talk about literally feeding off Chiho's generosity," Maou spat back.

"Um, I'm sorry," Chiho said, flustered, "I'll make some next time, so..."

"No need for you to concern yourself with it, Chi; it's nothing for you to worry about. Ever since he left the hospital, he's gotten more shameless than ever."

"Shameless? Oh, as if anyone cared how *I* was doing during and after my hospital stay! You all went crazy for Emilia's friends and Ashiya. You could at least give me a little something extra to eat, okay?"

"You aren't actually being serious, are you?"

In Maou's eyes, despite Urushihara's hospitalization, he hadn't undergone the sort of change debilitating enough to merit any particular concern.

"Are you serious, Maou? Like, hell, Amane and the landlord never even told me what I was being hospitalized for, right to the end. Don't you think something must've happened to my body for me to be there at all?"

"Well," Chiho tried, "all we can say is that Ms. Shiba's strange force had a negative effect on you...is all."

Apart from Shiba and her relatives, Chiho was the only one there to see Urushihara be taken to the hospital. She had set things up so that Urushihara could listen in on her asking Amane about Earth's Sephirah, but just as she was getting to the crux of it, Shiba had walked in, putting Urushihara into a coma and sending him off to treatment. If that treatment had been to heal his body after protecting Chiho and Suzuno from the archangel Camael's brutal attack on Chiho's high school, that would be one thing—but if the cause of any damage was simply "I ran into our landlord," it was hard to drum up much sympathy.

"Come on, I'm still losing my hair color any time she's nearby! Something's got to be messed up with me!"

"You've got too much hair on your head anyway. You could stand to lose some."

"I'm talking about the color, Maou, not the hair itself!"

"Oh, hush up. Losing your color, though… Did that ever happen to you, Laila?"

"No. It's been this color ever since you healed me a little while ago. Meeting with Ms. Shiba didn't change it at all."

Laila's hair had undergone the opposite transformation of Urushihara's. Originally a silvery shade of blue, it segued into an Urushihara-like purple hue right when Maou had used his demonic force to heal her wounds.

"The color's different, but it hasn't affected my health or anything."

"Yeah, and it didn't affect Urushihara's, either," Maou finished. "You're carrying on too much about that color, man. It's not like you willingly go outside anyway…ever. Just stay away from the landlord, and you're fine. It's not from the aftereffects of fighting Camael, either, so quit whining."

"Well, no," the dubious Urushihara replied, "but—"

"You say 'something extra to eat'! I hear it! Give up and open the door!"

The glutton on the other side of the door bellowed far louder than Urushihara, choosing to focus only on the parts of the conversation that meant the most to her. At a loss for any other solution, Maou stood up, bringing Chiho into the room as he stepped down to open the door.

"Whoo-hoo, Chiho— *Eek!*"

At that moment, the ravenous Acieth—mouth agape at all the edible gifts that Chiho didn't have for her—turned into a swarm of purple particles that were sucked into Maou's body.

"...In the house, please."

It was a rather forceful way of shutting her up but one that Maou and his fusion link with Acieth granted him unique access to.

"Ugh, all this racket... I'll let you out once we're done talking, so chill out for a while. Also, Chi's just back from work and she's tired. Don't give her any trouble!"

Maou winced and lectured Acieth, who was screaming at him at full volume in his mind, something that putting his hands to his ears wouldn't ease.

"Huh? Where's Acieth?"

But Acieth wasn't the only one outside. There was also Erone, his skin looking quite a bit healthier now, and, thanks to the Japanese clothing Nord and Laila bought for him, overall he appeared not at all different from any other neighborhood boy. Acieth *did* say "we" out there earlier—and now that Erone was tranquil and no longer "berserk" (as Laila and Amane put it), he was usually right by Acieth's side, manipulating Nord or Laila or Amane and forcing them to come up with the funds to satisfy both of their appetites. Today, though, the Sephirah child was clearly on the hunt for something, ferreting out the smell of Chiho (or the general MgRonald funk she had on her) and seeking a few freebies.

"You shouldn't hang out with Acieth all the time, either," Maou said to him, finger pointed at his own head. "You keep following behind her, and you'll start to act as brazen and pathetic as she does." Then he winced—no doubt Acieth yelling at him to "stop being so the rude" again, that much Chiho could tell.

"I don't want to go away from her, if I can," the boy suddenly blurted out. "We were separated for so long. Just getting to eat together every day... I still can't believe it. The past few days have been like a dream."

"Yeah, I can't believe how much you guys eat. And the funds we're going through for that aren't any dream at all. It's a cold, hard reality."

"Ah-ha-ha…ha-ha…"

Chiho had to laugh. She knew the extent of Acieth's and Erone's appetites all too well. But the chuckle subsided quickly as something occurred to her.

The two of them both had a seemingly insatiable hunger, but none of it had changed their bodies' shape at all. That was weird. The archangel Sariel—aka Mitsuki Sarue, erstwhile manager of the Sentucky Fried Chicken across the street from Maou's workplace—had attained a blimp-like appearance in very short order after getting smitten with Kisaki and subsequently living off nearly nothing but MgRonald value meals. It was obvious what eating so much fatty food should do to a body—either Sariel's or the Sephirah's—and even then, Sariel's gluttony was only a speck on the map compared to what Acieth and Erone were doing. They were absolutely stuffing themselves; it hadn't fattened them at all, and there had to be a reason for it.

Chiho tried to dismiss the vague concern from her mind, but the next words from Erone plunged her into a veritable ocean of worry.

"But if this isn't a dream, then this isn't any place for us to live."

"…!"

It may have been Chiho, or Maou, or both of them who gasped at the assertion.

"Acieth and Alas Ramus and I all have places we need to return to. But if I lose myself like I did before, I may never be able to go back."

"Don't say any more," Maou said, his voice suddenly stern. Erone ignored him.

"I have people I want to meet. I need you to lend me your power."

"I *said*, don't say any more."

"…Please, Erone, hold it back," Laila added, her voice low but sharp as she felt the danger lurking behind Maou's tone.

"All right. I'm sorry."

Following his apology, the boy bowed briskly at Maou, then did the same to Chiho, her face still tensed with anxiety.

"Sorry to you, too, Chiho. I've done nothing but scare you."

"Uh…ah…"

She wasn't scared at all, no. But the boy born from the Sephirah must have keenly picked up on the other kind of terror that was lurking deep in her heart.

"When we first met and later on, too. I have to protect people like you, Chiho, but look at me..."

"Protect...people like me?"

"I could never apologize enough to you, Chiho, but you always make such good food for me. You treat me so nice. And I...I'm trying to take these precious things from you, Chiho. I don't know what I should do."

"Erone...?"

"Will you quit it already—?"

"Oh! There you are!"

The voice of a harried-sounding Nord thundered up the outdoor stairway.

"I'm sorry. I took my eyes off him for a moment, and he ran off on me."

With all the lecturing Maou had given him lately, Nord was still having trouble figuring out exactly how to deal with his neighbors. He looked around the room.

"Did Acieth merge with you?"

"...Come on out."

"Agh!!"

It almost looked like the sour-faced Maou spat Acieth out, sending her reeling against the tatami-mat floor. She quickly picked herself up and turned toward Chiho.

"Chiho! I think you should give it the more thought!"

"Huh? More thought about what?"

"About Maou! You go in love with that man, you will receive the serious injury! If you marry Maou, it will be all of the trouble!"

The sudden *marriage* keyword took the already vaguely discomforted Chiho's mind and sent it well past the boiling point.

"Aaaaaaaaaaacieth?! What? Where did *that* come from?!"

"I mean it! You see, too, Chiho! When Maou feels— Oh no! I do not like this. He puts me in him! I promise you, all he say in future will be 'food, bath, sleep'! He is no good! Arrogant! And he will be ruling roost with *aghhggghh*!!"

Nobody had any idea where Acieth picked up this TV-sitcom

griping-housewife tone from. But just as it was starting to make Chiho's mind go in circles, there was a dull *thud*, followed by a weird and not at all Sephirah-like groan of pain.

"Ooh, that had to hurt," observed Urushihara.

"W-wait, Satan!" Laila added. "You should treat girls like Acieth better than that..."

The brisk, closed fist from Maou was enough to give both his plaintiffs instant pause.

"This is the only way I know to make kids who don't listen to reason sit down and shut up."

He then grabbed Acieth by the head and scruff, forcibly ejecting her from Room 201 and into Nord's arms, then slammed the door shut. Judging by the extended whining, cursing, and "I'm hungry!!" emanating from the corridor, Maou's tactic hadn't succeeded very much, but he ignored it all, locking and dead bolting the door and letting out a long-suffering sigh.

"...Sorry, Chi."

"H-huh?"

"Uh... Don't worry about it. Like, about what Erone and Acieth said."

"Oh, uh, o-okay."

Chiho nodded mechanically more than anything, her mind still racing. Seeing him sit down on the floor toward Laila again, she recalled why she came here in the first place and did the same, unzipping her coat to kneel down. That was why she couldn't say it—the question, heavy enough to have a physical presence, that made itself gently known in her mind as her brain cooled down. Right here, right now, it was a pointless query and really a doubt that meant nothing to anybody except her.

She knew why she was called here. She was witness to a conference between the Devil King and an archangel, covering topics that involved the fate of the human race on Ente Isla. Being asked for by name by Maou, a man she cared deeply for, was something she had to rejoice about. Being close to him, helping him, providing him strength—the perfect opportunity for all that.

So she swallowed the question, placing a lid over her complex, convoluted thoughts.

After all, in regard to Erone's and Acieth's words, what exactly was there *not* to worry about?

*

Despite being asked to accompany Maou and Laila in this talk, Chiho really had no idea what they'd be talking about.

Judging by the events around Urushihara's hospital bed, Laila probably wanted to enlist Maou and Emi's aid to help the Sephirah of Ente Isla out of their current crisis. Everything Laila had done up to now had to be driven by that, she knew, but when Chiho put everything she had learned together, it seemed like Laila was responsible for pretty much the whole bit—the young Maou becoming the Devil King Satan, and Emi being pitted against him as the Hero Emilia.

On Maou's side, the Yesod fragment that formed the mold for Alas Ramus. On Emi's, the one that formed her Better Half battle gear. The two of them clashing against each other should have been a great calamity for the people of Ente Isla—which should have been a cause of concern for both Laila and Miki Shiba, a woman closely involved with the Sephirah of planet Earth.

And Chiho herself, despite having nothing to do with Ente Isla, had an Ente Islan Yesod fragment of her own. She had lately taken to carrying it in a locked accessory case she bought to keep on hand at all times. A high school teen wearing a gaudy ring in public raised too many eyebrows, and the ban on jewelry at her job meant she almost never wore it anyway. Owning it once put her in mortal danger at the hands of angels, but between Maou, Emi, Amane, Shiba, and all the other forces protecting her, the heavens were no longer much of a threat.

Besides, given the place Chiho was granted with this ring and the person who did the granting, she had to surmise that Laila

and Gabriel—both apparently living in Japan long-term now—had their reasons for not wresting the ring back from her. Those Yesod fragments were at the core of the vast mystery Chiho had been staring at, and today that mystery was about to be solved.

"First," Laila said, "I want you to see this, Chiho."

"All right. Huh? Is that…? Huh?"

She reflexively looked at the item presented to her from the side. Her face had been deadly serious as she looked, pondering, but now her eyes were wide with surprise.

It was a plain old clear plastic file, blue in color, the kind you could find at any stationery shop or convenience store in Japan. Chiho took it from her like nothing was amiss, opened it up, then gave both Laila and Maou looks once she realized it.

This… This is just too crazy.

"Um… The crisis facing the world… Wow."

Could you really take all the dangers facing another world, another planet, and fit it in a standard letter-sized file, twelve pockets, straight from the hundred-yen shop?

The first page was the cover, the sort that'd lose out even to an ad flyer for a cultural studies course at the local community center in terms of flashiness. The title—"The Potential Danger to Ente Isla's Humanity Caused by Interference with the Tree of Sephirot"—was written in outlined characters that curved across the top of the page, a rainbow color gradient slapped over the white space below, and it had been printed notably off-center on the sheet.

"…Laila?"

"I tried working the layout so it'd be easy to read."

Chiho sighed at the angel, whose eyes were brimming with confidence at her own computer skills. This was, in its own way, dangerous. Any threat to humanity would involve a vast number of lives. Were rainbow colors and chunky letters *really* the way to go with this?

"Um, what do you call this stuff? This fancy 3-D lettering and design and so on?"

"WordArt," Urushihara replied. "From a really old version, too. I don't have any software that can do that, but I definitely think they upgraded all those designs for the current version."

"Oh, yeah, I think I learned this stuff on the really big computers they had in the AV room back in grade school..."

"That...that was brand-new technology back then!"

Faced with people as steeped in modern computer culture as Urushihara and Chiho, Laila suddenly felt less confident in her digital literacy. Her face reddened in shame. At least, Chiho reasoned, she knew now that this archangel, mother of the Hero of another world, had used her own PC to create this.

"It wasn't as cheap as what they have now and they weren't so easy to buy, but I worked hard to save up for my computer! I saved up a lot of money for my own family, too."

"It was, um, seventeen years ago when you first came to Japan, right, Laila? Back when the C drive on your average desktop had, what, two or four gigabytes?"

"Oh, I'm not using the exact same computer from seventeen years ago," Laila countered. "I replaced it around seven years later, so I got a sixty-gig hard drive and the newest business software suite they had at the time! And I've gotten to work with a lot of other computers, too!"

This wasn't exactly the debate everyone had come here to have. A ten-year-old business software suite would be an antique you'd have trouble even finding nowadays.

"Y'know, dude, it's practically criminal how much of an old model of notebook PC Maou got for me, but it's still got an eighty-gigabyte hard drive. If *your* computer's ten years old, they must've dropped support for the OS ages ago. It's dangerous to even use that thing."

"Oh, it's fine! It's not connected to the Net!"

Given her direct experience with the threat Laila's powers portended, it was difficult for Chiho to feel as close and casual with her as Maou and Urushihara seemed to be. But the sight of an archangel and fallen angel weighing the specs of their hopelessly outdated computers against each other still seemed oddly charming to her. Scenes like this were no longer any great surprise.

"So it's a decade-old computer with no Internet connection? What good is it then, dudette?"

"What's the big problem? If you're just browsing the Net, it's a lot easier with a smartphone anyway!"

Laila took her phone out from the bag she had placed in a corner of the room.

"Wow," marveled Chiho. "Like mother like daughter, huh?"

"Huh? How so, Chiho?"

"Oh, um, nothing..."

It seemed to her that the yawning abyss between Emi and Laila had narrowed just a bit in the days since the subway attack. Even so, Emi couldn't will herself to confront her mother, and Laila seemed lost about how to deal with her daughter, making both an agreement and any kind of parsable conversation an uphill battle. Calling them "mother and daughter" would be a joy for Laila to hear and a pain for Emi.

"It's just, you know, you really don't seem different from anybody else in the world, Laila."

"Really? Well, personally speaking, I'm happy to hear that. It's not like I set out to become an angel. I've always wished people could treat me more familiarly than that."

Laila seemed to treat Chiho's observation as a compliment. Urushihara did not.

"Yeah, well, I wouldn't be that happy. By that, y'know, she also means *I thought you lived up to your rep more, but you ain't nothing like what I thought*, so..."

"Urushihara!"

"What, am I wrong? You've never given a crap about being around angels and demons. You seriously asked me and Sariel if we were angels. Like, incredulously, to our faces."

"I—I didn't... Well, all right, maybe I did..."

"Yeah, but she's right to have done so."

"You too, Maou?!"

Urushihara was one thing, but having Maou join the choir gave Chiho a slight shock. Had she always been that sneering or sarcastic with them and maybe never realized it? The thought depressed her—but Maou's thoughts were slightly different from his fellow demon's.

"Well, I mean, Chiho's a lot stronger deep down than just in terms of her heart, or her feelings, or whatever. Demons like us, or angels like Sariel or Gabriel, aren't enough to make her fall to her knees in reverence or anything."

"Um, the angels are one thing, but I have a lot of respect for you guys, Maou!"

Despite her panic, Chiho still made it a point to exclude the angels from her appraisal. Maou couldn't help but laugh.

"Yeah, I appreciate the thought. Basically, what I'm saying is, you're perfectly fine being yourself, Chi."

"Ah—ah—ahhhhhhh..."

She was still panicked, unsure whether she understood Maou's intended meaning or not. Laila gave her a gentle pat on the shoulder as she half rose to her feet in a dither.

"It's all right. It's all right."

"Wha—wha—wha—wha—*what's* all right?"

"I know you don't think anything ill of me, Chiho, so...you know, you should read that report."

"That... Oh, right, this..."

Urushihara's passing remark had thrown the conversation far off course, but it all began because Laila had written this very non-angelic report on everything going on. Despite the distinct lack of critical danger the cover seemed to present, Chiho steeled her resolve and turned to the first page.

*

Once, there was a tree of life—a Tree of Sephirot—on Earth, along with the Sephirah born from it. As the Tree of Life nickname suggests, it was a gigantic growth, and it is fair to say that the Sephirah are its seeds, which eventually grow into similar trees. It is impossible to know for sure whether the Sephirots of Earth and Ente Isla are of the same species.

These trees only appear on planets whose animal life has sufficiently advanced into the realm of oxygen-breathing apes and other vertebrates. It sets up shop, parasite-like, on the moons or other celestial bodies closest to these planets, so as to have the maximum effect, and nurtures the creation of a civilization-bearing humanity from the hominids that call it home. A Sephirot does not have a cadre of chosen ones it decides to favor; instead, it basically facilitates the evolution of those people who have gained an unshakable position through the planet's long history of natural selection. There were other hominid races on Earth unrelated to modern mankind, but it wasn't that Earth's Sephirot eradicated them from the planet—if these other species had outclassed *Homo sapiens* and spread their influence planetwide, the Sephirot would have recognized them as "civilized" and not modern humans.

So what exactly *is* this tree, then, that attempts to cultivate civilized races? That, sadly, neither Laila nor anyone else from the heavens had an answer for. One thing they could provide, however, was a phenomenon observed from heaven once in the past. There had been a Sephirot that produced its so-called "last Sephirah," then released itself from its planet of its own biological will, vanishing into the nether regions of outer space. This was why nobody was sure whether Earth's and Ente Isla's Sephirot were the same in nature. Laila stated that evidence has been found for the remains of three past Sephirots at this point, but the only one currently active (as far as they knew) was the single one on Ente Isla.

Regardless, once a Sephirot picked the species it deemed worthy of further evolution, it gave birth to "children" to aid in their progress. These children of Ente Isla are the ten Sephirah: Kefer, presiding over thought and creativity; Chokhmah, over knowledge; Binah, over understanding; Chesed, over compassion; Gevurah, over strictness; Tiferet, over beauty; Netzach, over victory; Hod, over glory; Yesod, over foundations and spirits; and Malkuth, over the heavens and physical matter.

The role of these Sephirah is to come to the aid of mankind in the case of a danger to the entire race, in order to prevent a final, lethal destruction of the species. Thought, creativity, knowledge, understanding, and beauty all help in the quest to protect people from the illness and disasters that befall so many of them; victory and glory instill competitive spirit in them to help further polish their civilization; strictness and compassion both create and put an end to the wars that drive this competition; and the foundation, spirits, heavens, and physical matter help take all these individual members of a species and encourage them to behave as a cohesive unit.

The Sephirah are neither the guardians of mankind, nor some malevolent force interfering with their history. But when mankind faces the potential danger of extinction, something their civilization offers no way for them to avoid, they use their powers in all ways, shapes, and forms to keep them alive.

On Ente Isla, however, both the Sephirot and its Sephirah have had these abilities robbed of them. The angels in heaven have gained full control of the Sephirot, keeping its Sephirah exclusively for themselves. Having the heavens intervene between the people of Ente Isla and their Sephirah is what allows them to act as miracle makers, literal "servants of heaven," to mankind on that planet.

This has led to several adverse side effects. First, it has greatly slowed the advance of science and technology across all Ente Isla's intelligent people. It also led to them discovering the natural resources of demonic and holy energy. As can be seen from the vast similarities between humans on Earth and Ente Isla, Sephirots tend to latch on to planets that look a great deal alike. If Ente Isla had taken the path it was meant to take, it would have developed medicine to treat the ill, weapons to wage wars with, and science and technology to make people's lives easier, at a rate more or less close to Earth's. But with the heavens butting into the process, Ente Isla was losing the chances it had to discover or develop that tech for itself.

Instead, the angels used the powers they were originally gifted with to directly rescue Ente Isla's humanity from danger. Seeing these powers in action, the Ente Islans sought not to cultivate a process that would open perpetual growth and advancement to them but a way to copy these miraculous powers the servants of heaven showered upon them. This led to magic powered by holy force—and around the same time as the Ente Islans discovered the existence of holy force, the angels stopped paying regular visits to the planet's surface. This made mankind deify the angels, forming the cornerstone around which the Holy Church built itself.

Thus, the planet chose to advance its civilization by analyzing the nature of holy energy and weaving new magic that took advantage of it. But that led to serious problems. First off, unlike the Sephirah, the angels—and the heavens they dwelled in—had no inherent drive to keep the human race protected. The Sephirot/Sephirah system was built as a way to foster new civilizations; it would never ignore any potential threat to the species it had its eyes on. As had been seen over a long period of observing the heavens, the angels had no interest in taking on this role. Physically and deliberately, they have shown over the long string of years that their behavior did not match the Sephirah at all. To Sephirah eyes, it must have felt like a miracle that Ente Isla's humanity hadn't faced extinction yet.

The biggest issue of all, however, lay in how holy energy was not at all an unlimited resource. A Sephirot has the power to cultivate civilized species, but both it and its Sephirah are organic creatures and thus need to take in some form of energy to survive. This energy, to a Sephirot, was none other than the spiritual force housed within the species it chose. Much in the way a little water and nutrients in the soil can lead to astonishing crop growth in the right conditions, a Sephirot and its species existed in a form of symbiosis, extracting the energy both sides needed from each other.

That so-called holy energy, however, was now being expended across Ente Isla at an alarming rate. With magic at the very center of civilization, the rate of consumption was now far above the amount the planet's Sephirot would ever tap into.

"Spiritual force serving as energy..."

Chiho gasped a bit once she reached this point in the dossier.

The demonic energy Maou and his cohorts lived on, she knew, was driven from feelings of fear and despair in the minds of humanity. If this new revelation was to be believed, then the holy energy in Emi's and Suzuno's bodies—and her own as well—was the spiritual energy possessed by every man, woman, and child on Ente Isla.

What would happen if this was deliberately condensed and consumed in the form of holy energy? The answer was on the following page.

The predicted result of excessive holy energy usage is the withering of the planet's Sephirot and the subsequent death of its Sephirah. Ente Isla's humanity would lose its get-out-of-jail-free card for any lethal threats, and before long, its civilization would wane. They would no longer have the Sephirah protecting them from such threats, and the astonishing amount of holy energy driving their magic would irrevocably deplete the supply, tapping it fully and eventually making magic a thing of the past.

When that day came, it would mark the end of Ente Isla as a functional civilization. Even people like Emeralda, Albert, and Olba, capable of storing and accessing large amounts of holy energy, would eventually lose their stockpile and become...well, regular people. And with little scientific advancement to shore themselves up, the Ente Islans would have nothing to defend themselves within times of danger.

Even worse, holy energy was derived from the spiritual force within all humans; consuming too much of it would have effects that went far beyond a typical energy crisis. Following careful observation, Laila stated that birth rates across all five great continents that formed the "holy cross" of life on Ente Isla had gradually fallen over the past several centuries. Excessive holy energy consumption, she posited, may even hinder healthy births. This statistic formed much of the basis for Shiba's warning that Ente Isla could face a mortal crisis within another hundred years.

The planet, sadly, lacked the culture needed to create and keep worldwide statistics for itself. The Federated Order of the Five Continents, formed following the Devil King's Army invasion, still wasn't advanced enough to be capable of that. If anything, it was easy to imagine that the planet would come to rely even further on magic for rebuilding, developing, and prospering now.

That was why Laila believed that all the Sephirah have to be released as soon as possible. There was no taking back the past, but if they acted now and returned the Sephirot and Sephirah to their rightful positions, they might still be able to rescue Ente Isla's humanity from this crisis, albeit at a heavy cost likely.

In the way of this future, however, lay the heavens and its angels, forming a massive wall to block any progress. These angels hadn't captured the Sephirah just so they could act all high-and-mighty around the Ente Islans. Doing so provided them with several key advantages, in part thanks to the extremely long life spans and prominent force they wielded—but whether Laila would go into detail on this depended on whether Maou and Emi, now fully aware of the situation, agreed to help or not.

To sum up, Laila's mission was to release the Sephirot and Sephirah from heavenly rule, ensure the tree could give birth to its "final Sephirah," and guarantee Ente Isla's safety into the future. Achieving this meant resigning herself to a long, arduous string of battles. It meant making enemies out of a large chunk of heaven. But still, over a ponderously long time, Laila had been searching for someone or something powerful enough to take them all on.

*

"...All right. I see."

"And what do you think?"

Chiho, hearing the anticipation in Laila's voice, was unsure how to reply. She had no questions about what was written in the report. She was in pretty deep by now, having learned a great deal from her own experiences and what Amane and Shiba told her, and from that, there was a lot in Laila's testimony that made sense to her.

But if Ente Isla was in that much danger, it meant that within this cheaply bound printout, the fates of countless human beings hung in the balance. Considering that, the report certainly didn't seem very...*urgent* to her. She had at least a vague idea of Laila's concern and the issues facing Ente Isla, but it still all felt like someone else's problem. It was a bit dizzying to Chiho, like she was being shown a translated picture book detailing the myths and folklore of some foreign nation.

Laila had made an effort to keep the report accessible, even adding some schematics and other diagrams, but that wasn't what Chiho wanted. Chiho and likely Maou, too. It was important, yes, but none of this was enough for either of them to make a decision off. It hadn't really affected them emotionally at all.

"Um, may I ask something a bit odd?"

"..."

But rather than Laila, it was Maou that Chiho turned to. He gave her a silent nod—

"Oh, anything!"

—only to have Laila turn straight toward her, ready to take on the world if necessary.

"Well, then."

Chiho took a breath and returned her gaze.

"Laila…"

"Mm-hmm?"

"Are you working here in Japan at all?"

"………………………………………Huh?"

It was not a question anyone in the room could have predicted. Laila was the cleanup hitter, all crouched over in the batter's box and ready to swing for the fences, only to have the opponent's ace pitcher throw an intentional walk.

"Um…working?"

"Yeah."

"…Why do you ask?" Laila countered, her smile still painted on her face.

"Why? You said 'anything,' so…"

"I…suppose I did, yes…but why?"

"You're startin' to act really weird on us, Laila."

The angel was clearly disturbed by this line of inquiry, to the point that she ignored Maou's jab completely.

"No, um, I just started wondering as I was reading through this."

Her pupils now the size of dots, Laila's eyes moved toward Chiho, Maou, the back of Urushihara's head, then back toward Chiho.

"Well, not to answer your question with another question…"

"Oh?"

"But was that paper kind of hard to follow? Like, did it make you think about my work or my life here or…?"

"No," came the short reply. "That's exactly it. It didn't say anything about your own life, Laila, as far as I saw. That's why I started wondering."

"Ah…" Maou grinned a bit at this, understanding Chiho's point before Laila could. “You sure are kind to her, Chi. I wasn’t planning to say anything about that until she noticed it for herself.”

“Oh! Um, was that bad of me?”

Chiho, recalling Maou’s lack of enthusiasm for this whole discussion, gave him a concerned look. Maou grinned and shook his head.

“Nah. I doubt she’ll pick up on it anytime soon unless someone spells it out, so now’s as good a time as any.”

As the stupefied Laila looked on, Maou went up to his cheap plastic shelving and took out a piece of paper and a card case that not even Chiho had seen before.

“So here’s the draft version of the contract you gave me.”

“R-right.” Laila distractedly nodded as he presented the familiar sheet to her.

“If you were giving me something like this, I figured you were at least kind of aware, but seeing it, I doubt I’m gonna be interested in seriously hearing you out for a while to come.”

“Was—was there some kind of issue with it? Because I looked at a bunch of templates and bought a book about contracts and stuff…”

“It’s not about the content. Down here.”

He pointed at the bottom of the draft. It spelled out the names of Laila, executor of the contract, and Maou and Emi, its targets, including a little space to affix their seals to make it official.

“Isn’t something missing?”

Peering at the draft from the side, Chiho took a quick skim, immediately noticing what Maou was referring to.

“Laila, this… The addresses.”

“Um?”

“The addresses. There’s no place to write them.”

“Ad…dress?” She made a face like this wasn’t in her vocabulary. “Did—did you need that?”

“Of course we do! What are you saying?”

Laila looked shocked at this. It almost hurt Chiho a bit; if anything, she reasoned, *she* had a good reason to be shocked. Even a teenager who hadn’t worked with anything besides a labor contract for her part-time job knew that any valid contract in Japan needed three things: names, addresses, and official seals. Laila was trying to sign a contract with Maou that included promises of rewards later on, and yet she had failed to even provide a space for addresses. It went far beyond the realm of a careless error.

"I'm not going to break this contract or anything," Laila doggedly exclaimed. "Besides, it's not like we can take this to Japanese court if either side has a problem, is it? All we need here is our names and a common agreement..."

Chiho could already imagine the two of them in a courtroom.

"I agreed to save an entire world from danger, but she never provided me her promised payment!"

"I provided the exact compensation we agreed to, Your Honor!"

"But a single payment for all the Sephirah is ridiculous, considering all the work it took to release all of them!"

"All of that was factored in the final agreement, Your Honor, right up to the maximum predicted level of difficulty!"

"Pfft!"

She couldn't help but laugh out loud, especially when she imagined Reconciliation Panel chairwoman and Room 202 resident Suzuno Kamazuki in the judge's chair.

"N-no, Laila, that's not what Maou is talking about."

"So...what, then?"

"Chiho Sasaki just said it, dude. We're all normal people here, but from our perspective, you're still an *angel*, Laila."

"Lucifer?"

Maou nodded. "Exactly. I don't know where you live, you know?"

Bewildered, Laila blinked at this.

"Stuff happening on Ente Isla is one thing," Maou said as he looked at the draft contract, then the doomsday report placed next to Chiho. "But I don't know a single thing about where you live in this country, how you're putting food on the table, and how you plan to be involved with Japan going forward."

Then he opened the case he took from the shelf, placing several small cards from it on the tatami floor.

"My name is Sadao Maou. I live in Villa Rosa Sasazuka, Sasazuka city, Shibuya ward, Tokyo. Around here, I'm a human being."

One card was Maou's driver's license, complete with photograph so embarrassing that he steadfastly refused to show it to anyone at first.

"This is my national health insurance card. This is my official seal registration I submitted to the Shibuya Ward Office. Any info about my work history is probably kept at MgRonald's main Tokyo HQ. How much proof can *you* provide that you exist in this world?"

"That I exist…here…?"

Having all these tools to prove Maou's identity thrust before her left Laila unable to do anything but stare at the floor.

"Because right now, you're still an angel to us. Someone who might appear or disappear at any time, just like you did before. Not a human who has an actual *life* here."

Being declared not human made Laila blanch a bit.

"I mean, look at Sariel. He goes by Mitsuki Sarue here in Japan, and he's still an angel and an enemy to me. But he works right nearby, and as much as I hate to think about it, he lives in what's apparently a pretty nice apartment. He was blowing tons of cash trying to impress my manager way back when, so I know he's comfortable financially. The way he tries to butter up any woman he sees grosses me out, but it seems like he and his staff get along pretty well. He's used to life in Hatagaya—to the point where he agreed to keep our shopping area safe if something happened while me and Suzuno were in Ente Isla saving Emi's hide."

He may have been an enemy—in terms of bloodlines, destinies, and fast-food rivalries—but even Maou had at least one or two good things to say about the archangel.

"And you know, along those lines, if *he* was the one who brought this up with me, maybe I would've lent a more serious ear to it, you know?"

"Huh?!" Laila looked shocked. "I'm below Sariel…? That much?"

"If I could go into more detail, I feel like Sariel would have come up with kind of a clearer report, too. He's got experience making employee manuals and flowcharts and stuff."

Chiho's follow-up was like a fatal torpedo to Laila's defense.

"Yeah. And it's not like I trust his type at all. We aren't in regular contact or anything. But as long as Ms. Kisaki is working in Hatagaya, I'm one hundred percent positive he isn't moving an inch from there. Even if his company decides to transfer him somewhere else, I'm pretty confident he'll tap into his archangel forces to keep himself there if he has to. But even with that, he's living a regular life here in Japan that's been accepted by dozens, if not hundreds, of people around him."

"He was awful to me at first, too," added Chiho, "but with everything that's happened since, we say hello to each other nowadays when we pass by in the shopping arcade."

"Yeah, dude, he certainly showed us how much of a hard worker he is. That was a surprise, huh?"

Even Urushihara was willing to give this honest assessment, having seen how he stepped up while Maou and Suzuno were gone from Earth.

"Mmm. But what about *you*, huh? I have no clue where you live or where you're getting your money from. You're showing up a lot more often than you used to, but if you flake out again, we've got no way to track you down. Considering that, what if something happens to Emi or Nord and you never show up? 'Cause that seems entirely possible to me."

"N-no, I'd never—"

"And you *know*, I'm sure Emi would say the same thing. If you asked me, after all the scheming and conniving you've done around us, I still don't really know why you've picked this moment in time to show yourself. I know you're kinda part of the Devil's Castle dinner club now, but don't think we're just letting that slide forever."

"I... That..."

Laila looked downward, her guard weakening now that Maou had finally gotten his point across to her.

"You know, you've everything worked out in terms of appearances, but you're still dealing with us in bad faith. Like you always have. Enough to make me wonder if you're providing all this info, like the story bible for some TV show, so you can keep the wraps over your own situation in case you feel the need to slip away again. And all this stuff's so vague, too. There's too little meat to it."

"I...I'm sorry...?"

"So, really, in the end, I'm kind of forced to question how much of this whole story is true, y'know? Because there's nothing in here I'm willing to believe in so much that I'll close my eyes to the fact that you angels are still our enemy. Whether whatever you're doing is really the best thing for the future of Alas Ramus and all the rest or not."

"..."

"Laila..."

Chiho patted the shoulder of the silent, downtrodden angel.

"It's all right. Chiho," the woman replied, brushing the hand away. "I'm sorry. You're right. You warned me about that in Lucifer's hospital room, and I'm just doing the same thing over again, aren't I?"

"You've gotten so used to being a social outcast, it must've soaked into your brain by now, huh?"

"There, you see, Laila? Even Urushihara feels valid saying stuff like that to you. Shouldn't you be ashamed of yourself?"

"Oh, Maou!"

"It's fine. I can't defend myself against it. Besides..."

"Hmm?"

Laila lifted her face a little, then turned it a bit to the side toward Urushihara.

"I'm...partly at fault for what happened to Lucifer anyway."

Here, for the first time, was something that honestly piqued both Maou's and Chiho's curiosity. Their eyebrows arched up.

"What?"

"Huh?"

Urushihara gave Laila a deeply unpleasant stare. "Uh, dude, could you not phrase it so you sound like a mom apologizing for the way she raised her kid? 'Cause that burns, man."

"But, Lucifer—"

He shook his head before she could continue. "I really don't care. Like, really, I don't even remember much of it. How long ago d'you think that was?"

"Yeah..."

Then he turned back toward his computer and fell silent. Laila turned a pair of saddened eyes toward his back. It made Maou and Chiho feel eminently uncomfortable.

"Y'know, Chi, that sounds like something that's gonna take the squabbling among Emi's family and throw it in one damn crazy new direction."

"No, it certainly didn't seem like a laughing matter to me..."

Urushihara and Laila looked at them, one fully understanding how Maou and Chiho interpreted their conversation just now and the other not at all.

"Dudes, don't get the wrong idea. 'Cause depending on how you interpret it and who's doin' the interpreting, it'd mean both my life and the lives of, like, a bunch of others."

"Huh? What do you mean?"

""Um, nothing,"" Maou and Chiho awkwardly said in unison, faces turned away.

"But...all right. I understand. So listen, Satan—and you too, Chiho, if you like."

"Hmm?"

"What is it?"

"I'd like you two to forget all about this for now," Laila said, taking the doomsday report from Chiho's hands. She sat back down, looking them straight in the eye. "If you like, you can come visit my place. My home in Japan, of course."

"Your..."

"Your home?"

Chiho looked bewildered. Maou lowered his brows in disbelief.

Laila gave them both a firm nod. "Right. I've lived at several addresses since I came to Japan, but I've been at the same place for five years now. My work keeps me away from home some nights, though."

Whether her "work" meant her efforts related to this doomsday report or the answer to Chiho's question wasn't clear at this point.

"But over there, you'll find a lot more than this report. You'll see all the resources and information I've collected worldwide over centuries. There's documents, talismans, devices you won't find anywhere except heaven. If I wanted to...I could even make angel's feather pens for you, Satan...and Emilia, and Chiho. Everyone here. It will take some time, but..."

"You mean...!"

Laila's casual reference to a familiar item shocked Chiho and even made Maou raise his eyebrows. Creating such a pen required a feather from the wings of an archangel, allowing the user to freely create Gates without any need for magic casting. As an archangel herself, Laila probably could craft more than a few. Shiba stated that the heaven of Ente Isla had firmly shut its borders, impossible to access even via a Gate—but if Laila could gift a stock of feather pens for Maou and everyone else, that was an enticing offer, whether it involved freeing the Sephirah or not. Plus, these were Laila's feathers. If she decided to vanish again, they could probably use them to find her.

Chiho gave Maou an expectant look. After all this waiting and talking it out, they finally had something concrete to work with. Maou answered her expression with a reply that came quicker than she expected.

"I'd be willing to go now, if you want."

""Wha?!"" exclaimed both Chiho and Laila.

"But you probably gotta get home, huh, Chi? It's getting late."

"Oh, um..."

"Ah, er..."

Both women were stammering at the same time.

"...Something wrong with that, you two?"

""N-no, um, I'm not ready,"" the archangel and teenager echoed in unison.

"Not ready?" Maou gave Laila an exasperated sigh. "*You're* the one who invited us."

Laila put her hands together, bowing her head to Maou. "I-I'm sorry. I really do want you to come visit, but I didn't expect you to ask for right *now*, so, um, maybe sometime besides today?"

"Why? You got plans or something tonight? Emi's working until ten PM, I think, so you won't be seeing her."

"Um, no, not that, but..."

"Wait," Maou rumbled. "Don't tell me Emi doesn't know your home address, either?"

""!!""

Another synchronized gasp from the two women. Their subsequent reactions, however, diverged from there—Laila averting her eyes from Maou, but Chiho scowling and turning her head downward.

"I, um, actually, I haven't been able to talk about stuff like this with Emilia at all..."

"Come *on*, lady!" Maou's eyes burst open at Laila and her penchant for constantly making excuses. "You *still* haven't? How many days has it been?"

It had been over a week since Maou and Emi proclaimed an interest in working with Laila.

"Well, not like this, okay? I'm not going to your place before Emi does. I doubt she'd bring it up with me, but I guarantee she'll be upset with you all over again."

It was near the end of the year. Everyone was busier than usual. But she *still* hadn't found an opportunity to talk things over with Emi? Maou began to wonder which side was the main cause of that.

"Y-yeah. I know. I want to discuss matters with Emilia, and...and that's another reason why we can't do it today! I'm sorry about that! If it's tomorrow...ooh, maybe the day after, actually..."

"The day *afterrrr*?"

The disbelief was obvious from Maou's nasal reply as he glanced at the monthly work schedule tacked to the refrigerator.

"Hmph. Lucky us, huh? Me, Chi, and Emi aren't scheduled for anything that evening. That's pretty rare, you know. Day after tomorrow, you got it?"

The day fell on a weekday, but by sheer coincidence, the three of them weren't scheduled for anything beyond the start of evening.

"I, um, I'll try."

It was a rather odd reply to Maou's declaration. But at least it marked this mystery woman Laila promising to remove at least one layer of the veils surrounding her.

"Also, while I have the chance, can you give me your phone number? 'Cause seriously, you make me anxious. I gotta get as much info outta you as I can while you're still here."

"All right."

Laila meekly took out her smartphone, opened her contacts list, and provided it to Maou. He typed Laila's number into his, double-checking to ensure he got it right, then had Chiho do the same before tossing the phone back at the archangel.

"Oh, and try talking to Emi for a change, too, all right? We'll share the contact info with her, but don't assume we can easily reach her anytime of day."

Laila meekly nodded at the sharp warning. "...I'll try on that, too."

Just as it looked like things were wrapping up, Urushihara turned back around.

"So what're *you* 'not ready' for, Chiho Sasaki?"

"............Oh, uh, yes."

She had acted a bit thrown at first, but now that they had a firm promise to meet at Laila's residence, Chiho had started to show signs of calm. Maou worried that it wasn't calm so much as depression.

"Chi?"

But she shook her head at him. "No, um, I'm all right. The question got settled as we were talking."

"Oh? Well, good."

"Are you coming, too, Chiho? Lucifer's invited, too, if he likes, and Alciel and Bell..."

"Oh, um, I'll ask," Chiho replied, the tone of her voice low.

"No thanks, dude. Sounds too much like work. Not like I'll have anything to do over there."

As the entire human race could have predicted, Urushihara turned down a chance to venture outside.

"Yeah, so... I dunno if having the whole gang over would be all that great, but I'll go ahead and ask Ashiya and Suzuno. See you in two days. My shift's till five, but I'll contact you about a meetup time once we know what Chi's school schedule looks like."

"A-all right."

Laila's speech had been oddly wooden for a while now.

"Do you think we should invite Nord and Emeralda, too, Maou?"

"Yeah... Emeralda I dunno, but Nord for sure..."

Judging by the way Laila put it, Nord had never seen the place, either, whether he knew about its existence or not. If it was just Emi going, that was one thing—but ignoring Nord even after nonfamily members like Maou and Chiho were invited wouldn't be very kind.

Adding him to the mix seemed like a completely normal gesture to make, but for some reason, it made Laila visibly wince.

"No! Not him!!"

"Huh?" "Oh?" "Dudette?"

This was a surprise for all three of them.

"Look, whether you want him or not, he's kind of important..."

Maou was honestly bewildered. Nord was Laila's husband. Maou, on the other hand, wasn't related to either of them. Why was *he* okay but Nord off the list?

"Y-yes, um, I know full well how weird this sounds. I know, but, um, he, uh, if *he's* coming, too, then I dunno about two days from now..."

"Quit talkin' nonsense." Maou looked at the December shift schedule on the fridge and winced. "If it's not two days, then I don't see another time when we're all free for a while!"

"I—I know, I know. I'm well aware it's my fault for letting this go for so long. It's my crime. But it's all right. I'll figure something out. He might say no for all I know, so, um, yeah, day after tomorrow. That's fine."

Allowing Satan, King of All Demons, to come as she excluded her own husband seemed ridiculous. But Maou held back. Haranguing Laila about this could make her call the whole thing off.

"All right. So...where should we go in two days, Laila?"

"Oh, right, right. Yes. Umm, Shinjuku. Can we meet up at Shinjuku station, maybe? I'll be taking the Oedo Line, so how about by the turnstiles at the Keio Line west exit?"

"All right."

It was a familiar spot. Chiho often used it as a meetup site for outings with her own friends.

"Satan?"

"Sure."

"I, um, I'll tell him about my home myself. I think I should really be the one to tell him, so..."

"Yeah. Tell Emi, too. Don't forget her."

"...All right."

Laila had practically broken into a cold sweat from the moment Nord's name came up, but she still had enough composure to nod at the stony-looking Maou.

"..."

Meanwhile, Chiho simply looked on, a melancholy smile on her face.

"Whew... Sure has gotten cold."

Chiho was walking alone across Sasazuka at night, on her way home. Maou offered to accompany her, but she turned him down. She'd normally bite at every chance to spend time with him she got, but today, she didn't want to be alone with him. Laila sounded like she still had things to talk about, and besides, the city was bustling enough at this time of night that being by herself wasn't dangerous. There was no reason for angels or demons to attack Japan at the moment, and Erone, the cause of all that trouble a bit ago, was safe and sound.

Right now, there was nothing to be concerned about, and no need to cause trouble for Maou. That was one reason. The other one—

"Maou sure is nice to her..."

The words, whispered softly enough to avoid entering anyone's ears, floated in her white breath for a moment before disappearing from anyone's sight.

If Laila had been okay with it, Chiho was perfectly willing to head for her house right this moment. But when the topic came up, the first thing that flashed in Chiho's mind was Emi. Her motivations for concern were the same as Maou's over Nord. Was it really all right, Laila ignoring her own daughter and letting a stranger like Chiho into her place? That was what she found herself not ready for.

No matter how thick and sturdy a wall Emi had built between herself and Laila, the archangel had to find a way to climb over it and fill in the gap, at least a little. If someone else learned of Laila's location before Emi did, and she found out about it, her feelings were bound to be hurt. It'd make her act even more obstinate around her mother. And beyond worlds being in danger and all that, as Emi's friend, Chiho absolutely wanted to keep that from happening.

But she couldn't go right out and say that. That's because Chiho was under the same incorrect assumption as Maou—the reliability, or lack thereof, of Laila. Maou worried that if he turned this offer down, he'd lose any chance of approaching her again. But right after Chiho hesitated over the question, Maou had said it himself: *Not like this, okay? I'm not going to your place before Emi does.* He showed care for Emi's feelings. *I doubt she'd bring it up with me, but I guarantee she'll be upset at you all over again.* Maybe he didn't mean it, but the words seemed to strike a chord with Laila, suggesting that doing so would be the best thing for both her and Emi.

"Kind of nice, I guess..."

Since returning from Ente Isla, Maou had expended every effort possible for Emi's sake—all in an effort to make her feelings, her work, and her relationships that little bit better. Maou would deny it all, of course, claiming "No way—even if it looks that way, I'm doing it all for *me*," or whatnot. But to Chiho—and really, you didn't need to ask Chiho to know this—the more she saw Maou acting so naturally human, the more it had to be just that—*naturally human*. It was said that compassion for the plight of others was its own reward, but to turn that around, doing good things for *yourself* could help out other people, too.

"I hope Yusa and Laila make up, though..."

It was a purely Chiho kind of hope—and as she figured it, the time wouldn't be too far into the future. Emi had yet to make an approach from her end, sadly, but with Maou intervening, the chasm separating her from Laila was gradually starting to fill in. That was reflected in the way Laila was intruding on Devil's Castle dinners or even in the passing words and behaviors Emi showed during her job at MgRonald.

Emi might deny it all, just like Maou did—deny that Maou was bending over backward to help her. But Chiho knew. In recent days, Emi had given Maou more smiles, far more in fact, than she ever did before.

"...Oh, man..."

She hated thinking along those lines. But the more she tried to deny the thoughts her own brain created for her, the more Urushihara's passing remark put her mind in the blender.

By that, y'know, she also means I thought you lived up to your rep more, but you ain't nothing like what I thought, *so...*

Nothing like what I thought. It sounded petty of her, and she didn't want to think she was capable of being mean. But she wasn't confident that it *wouldn't* look like that, depending on how it was received. And, you know, maybe it *wasn't* like what she thought, kind of. For ages now, Chiho had wanted Maou and Emi to get along—no bile, no killing, just find a landing point for their feelings and make a clean break from their bitter past in Ente Isla. That was what she had always wanted from the heart, and now that desire was taking form before her eyes.

And yet...

"Why, though...?"

Why were there all these butterflies in her stomach? She wanted this for all of them—even now, from the bottom of her heart. She was happy. But behind that happiness lurked deeper, darker feelings. And whenever Emi smiled at Maou, whenever Maou did something thoughtful for Emi, those feelings did their best to kick away that happiness and rule over her.

"Ugh."

It's not turning out like I had hoped for.

"I hate this."

Nothing like it.

"Why am I...?"

Nothing.

"This total...!"

"Chiho!"

"Chi-Sis!"

"...?!"

Chiho's face darted upward at the familiar voices greeting her from the front of Sasazuka station up ahead. She had instinctively blocked her face from them, attempting to quell her darkly brooding heart in the night, and was gritting her teeth as she walked.

Recognizing them, she attempted a natural smile, only to feel all the muscles in her face tense up.

"Oh, Suzuno and Alas Ramus..."

The voice coming up to her definitely belonged to Suzuno Kamazuki from Room 202. But—

"Huh?"

She looked different from normal. Chiho couldn't believe her eyes at first. The dark feelings from moments ago dissipated in a flash.

She couldn't help but rub her eyes at the sight. But Suzuno kept walking up to her, Alas Ramus in tow, looking the same as when Chiho first caught sight of her.

"Hiiiii, Chi-Sis!"

"Returning from the apartment, perhaps? Laila was there, was she not?"

"Um, yeah, she was, but... Um, *what*?"

Suzuno and Alas Ramus were both sporting reddened cheeks in the cold.

"Rare to see you so bundled up like that, Chiho. Certainly well prepared for visiting the apartment building, I will admit."

"You look like Relax-Beaw, Chi-Sis!"

Chiho couldn't even smile politely at Alas Ramus's unintended sarcasm. Her large, round eyes were still set firmly upon Suzuno.

"Ahhh—ah—ahhhhh, um, Suzuno?"

"I went out to catch the evening sale at the grocery store, but do you know, Chiho, of the store in the shopping arcade that constantly changes its merchandise in and out, like a bazaar of some manner?"

"Y-yes..."

"They had the most fetching hairpin on sale there. Look at this! It has a snow crystal that looks like a cross. I simply *had* to have it, and I was soon wandering up and down the shops. Before I knew it, heavens be, look at how late it had become!"

"Look, look! Suzu-Sis gave dis to me!"

Alas Ramus was wearing an unfamiliar (to Chiho) wool hat. She was now eagerly showing the top of her forehead to the teen, as if about to head-butt her.

"Ooh, um, neat. It looks good on you. Really good. But, um, I'm sorry, Alas Ramus, can you give me a second?"

"Ooh?"

There was something tensed up about Suzuno, clutching her recyclable shopping bag in one arm and Alas Ramus's hand with the other. They were both excited. Perhaps the thin belt-type wristwatch on Suzuno's left hand had something to do with it.

"Um, I'm sorry, Suzuno, this might be kind of a weird question..."

"Hmm?"

"Wh-why are you dressed like that?"

"Oh? Oh, ah, this?" Suzuno blushed a little, as if only now noticing what she had on. "I chose this outfit by myself. It's not overly strange, is it?"

"N-no, no, you look great. I'm just really surprised, you know, Suzuno..."

Chiho's eyes ran up and down Suzuno's body, as rude as she knew that must have been.

"I mean, you wearing nothing but, ah, modern clothes..."

She still had an ornate hairpin as the final touch for her long hair, but underneath her gray poncho was a white shirt and a short-length navy-blue dress; thick, tight leggings; and short, fringed boots covering her legs.

"You saw how cold it grew now, yes? The daytime temperature had been high enough as of late that I procrastinated on changing out my wardrobe, and then it came all too suddenly, as it does. It even snowed the other day."

"It...it sure did..."

"I was positively freezing, what with the kimonos I have on hand."

"Yeah..."

"They say the *kasuri* splash-pattern kimonos are useful enough for wear in the winter, but the sleeves are still wide open, you see. Even with a heavy undershirt, one will still feel a chill in the shoulders, and it would do little to solve the sleeve issue. Plus, you know the kind of apartment I live in, yes? Not to criticize Ms. Shiba's generosity, but even with a heater, the cold reaches one's bones if one isn't careful."

"I can understand that."

Chiho could picture it perfectly, hence her multiple layers.

"So I made up my mind to shop for more clothing, and this Western wear was cheaper and warmer."

She had no idea what a *kasuri* was, but apparently the combination of cold weather and low prices made Suzuno bend her kimono-only rule a bit.

"So perhaps I may rely on clothing like this for day-to-day needs, yes. But if something happens and my services are needed, I do intend to retain my kimono as battle gear. This ponk...ponch...ah, what was it called...?"

"Poncho?"

"Yes. That. This gray poncho. It functions just fine when draped over a kimono as well. I have grown used to life here in Japan by now, so I thought that perhaps I should learn to liven up my wardrobe with an East-meets-West philosophy."

"Yeah, you look really cute in that, Suzuno."

This was Chiho's first look at Suzuno in modern wear since her and Emi's tandem birthday party. Seeing her here, in clothing that allowed her to completely blend in with the modern Japanese cityscape, to Chiho she looked like a bright young woman in her prime (not that she knew her actual age).

"Have you been wearing stuff like this for a while?"

Chiho had last encountered Suzuno only about three days ago, when she was still in her familiar kimono gear.

"I finally succumbed to the cold and went out to purchase Western gear the day before yesterday. I only have a couple of outfits yet, but I am still debating whether to purchase more or stick with the kimono. Thanks to that, I have wound up giving Alas Ramus quite the window-shopping tour around town. You must be tired by now, are you not?"

"I'm okeh!"

Much about Alas Ramus's stamina and physical strength remained an enigma, but for now, keeping up with an adult going store hopping hadn't made her bored or fatigued at all. Plus, Chiho was taken too far out of her comfort zone to notice, but the wool hat Suzuno bought for her featured the same *kamawanu* scythe-laden cloth pattern as some of Suzuno's own kimonos. She found it pretty funny.

"It must've been quite a leap for you, Suzuno."

Seeing Suzuno emphasize repeatedly that her passion for Japanese clothing hadn't waned at all was almost as funny to her, too. Modern wear really *did* look nice on her, though. Chiho hoped her friend would take this opportunity to explore Western fashion a bit more.

"Indeed it was! And when that cursed Devil King saw me in the corridor, he looked at me like I was a monster."

"Maou did?"

"Yes. On first glance, he said, 'Did this winter give you a fever or something?' Rather rude, would you agree?"

Kind of a harsh jab. People talk about the summer heat driving them nuts, but catching a cold and running a fever in the winter was far from unheard of.

"Of course," Suzuno continued as Chiho thought about this, "he *did* agree that it looked good on me, so I let it slide."

"He said that?"

"Indeed." She grinned. "Rather reluctantly, but he did."

The smile made a wave of darkness crash over her heart again, just as it did when she tried hiding her face to quell the sensation.

"Wow… Maou…"

"Mm?"

"N-no…"

But letting someone else learn about this wave of emotion didn't strike her as a good idea. She shook her head, letting the night hide the hardened lines of her expression. Suzuno seemed to pay it no mind, her eyebrows suddenly furrowing at the sight of something behind Chiho.

"Still, as little need for concern as we may have right now, the Devil King having you go home at night alone strikes me as rather thoughtless."

"Huh? Oh, it wasn't that…"

Wait…?

"The city can pose any number of hazards that have nothing to do with any angel or demon, as you know. Though I suppose it is rather ridiculous in itself, the way said angels and demons have caused you so much danger..."

This is weird.

"If you are traveling directly home, Chiho, I could join you."

"...N-no, no, it's fine."

"I am not in a hurry. Besides, we do this all the time, do we not?"

Something about me today...

"I'm...I'm fine."

"...Chiho?"

"Chi-Sis?"

I'm just messed up.

"I..."

I hate this, but...

"What—what is the matter? What happened?!"

Suzuno half panicked at the sudden turn of affairs, looking up at Chiho from below.

"I-I'm telling you, I'm fine...!"

Tears were flowing. And as Chiho thought, they couldn't have been flowing for reasons any more trivial, any more ridiculous, than hers. But they just wouldn't stop.

"Well, I mean, the Devil King... Yes, the Devil King in particular would never do anything strange to you, Chiho, and you appear unhurt. Is it...*him*?! Lucifer?! Oh, what insensible act has he done this time...?"

"Chi-Sis, you hurt? You hurt? How much? You hurt? How much?"

The sight of Chiho standing there and crying out of nowhere made Suzuno flail about for an explanation and Alas Ramus rap at her knees with her tiny hands, as if trying to knock the pain out of her.

"I-I'm sorry, I'm sorry..."

"Well, all right, for now calm yourself, Chiho, I...I know! There is a café in the train station; um, I am not sure what happened, but it is cold out here. All right? So let's go inside and drink something warm..."

The level of panic was uncharacteristic for Suzuno as she motioned Chiho to head with her into Sasazuka station.

Just as Chiho and Suzuno were entering the Tacoma's Best coffee shop under the tracks:

"Oh dear, it's so late. I'm sure Ms. Sasaki is back home by now."

A harried young man tore out from near the turnstiles, rubbing his frigid hands.

"I hadn't expected the phone call to run for so long. Ahh, it's so chilly!"

The tall form of Shirou Ashiya, carrying a recyclable bag filled with his assorted evening purchases, sped its way out from the station.

*

"Mornin', Saemi!"

"Oh, good morning, Akiko."

It was customary in the Japanese language to say "good morning" when greeting someone at the beginning of a shift, even if it was actually six PM, like it was now.

Emi was on from noon to ten that day, and MgRonald veteran Akiko Ohki had caught her just as she wrapped up her predinner break. She was the same age as Kawata, but she had joined the Hatagaya crew a good half year later, and she was a year behind him in college. As she put it, she figured studying for college exams would be easy, found out otherwise, and took a year off to prepare.

The end of November was usually a busy period in the Japanese college year, so Akiko was running on a reduced schedule. Emi hadn't seen her in about a week.

"Hey, Saemi," Akiko called as she changed into her uniform.

"Yeah?" Emi asked as she put a book she was reading into her locker.

"You used to work somewhere else, didn't you? Like, office-type stuff?"

"Yeah, I worked at a Dokodemo call center."

"Whoa, really? How long?"

"About a year and a half, I think. I had some family stuff come up so I had to take off for a while, and they basically tore up my contract."

Being held prisoner in an alien world and forced to wage a massive war against legions of unearthly demons was, if you didn't mind skipping a lot of the details, "family stuff" in Emi's mind. But it was the mention of a contract that made Akiko wrinkle her eyebrows.

"Oh, man, firing you for stuff that's not your fault? That's mean. But you lasted a year and a half, huh? 'Cause I flamed out after, like, two months."

"You've worked at a call center before?"

"Yeah. Outcalls mostly."

"Ooh. I was usually doing support."

Call center jobs could be broadly classified into one of three categories. Emi worked at an in-call site, which fielded questions from customers. She didn't know what kind of job Akiko had, but if it involved outcalls, it probably meant selling products or taking orders from people. Some companies were involved with both at the same time, too.

"You know how we'll lose Kota soon, right? That kinda reminded me a lot of the stuff I did on that job."

"Mm-hmm?"

"I mean, I knew in advance that call center jobs are tough, but my first job was with kind of a big educational company. We were mostly dealing with the mothers of small children, right? I figured there wouldn't be anything too scary about them."

"...You didn't think so at *first*, I bet."

Emi grinned. She could see where this was going.

"Yeah. One time, when I was just starting out, this old man called with a question and told me I'm the reason why Japan is going down the toilet."

"Wow. Pretty big leap in logic."

Akiko nodded without going into further detail. "It's like...I don't know, the more normal someone is, the more extreme their mood swings and stuff can be. Like, I almost liked it better if they started the call all angry or peeved, because maybe they'll yell at ya, but you can still deal with them."

Emi had a memorable sequence of screaming and lecturing along these lines once, from another elderly person who put the entire weight of Japan's future upon her shoulders. The general flow: Modern electronics have to stop leaving older people in the lurch like this. → You young people are so focused on these gadgets, Japan's manufacturing is spending its money on nothing but heavy industry and electronics. → It's deplorable how young people think they know everything about the world through their little phone screens. → And there's so much poverty in rural areas, and agriculture is about to fall apart. → You should be ashamed of yourself, working for a company that's screwing Japan so badly. → Why don't you try going outside for a change. → See, you're exactly why this country's going to hell in a handbasket!

All this over the course of around three hours.

She wasn't the sort, of course, to let irrational insults and shouting faze her, but the exchange stuck in her mind even now, partly because it happened early on when she wasn't used to the work and partly because she never *did* figure out what the customer even called for. The guy just hung up after extracting a promise from Emi that she'd vote in the next general election. Fortunately, that was a pretty extreme example, setting the standard for epic calls across the office for a while afterward—to the point that the floor leader and several of Emi's friends, Rika Suzuki included, treated her to dinner for it.

"So, you know, at the time, it really depressed me. Like, am I ever gonna find a job or anything? It's easy enough when you're dealing one-on-one with customers in person, but if I'm at a desk with a phone, it's gonna be such a trauma dealing with those calls, I bet. I guess you and Ms. Kisaki are used to it enough that you can run the phone orders here, though, huh?"

"Well, keep in mind, you always remember the craziest calls because they were so crazy. Ninety-nine percent of them are nothing like that. I'm sure you've taken a lot of normal calls, too, Akiko, so I bet you'll be fine."

"Yeah, I know, but it's kinda hard to forget being called a murderer just because you're trying to sell teaching materials, y'know?"

Emi was sincerely curious about the sequence of events leading to that, but the minute hand on the clock was dangerously close to the end of her break, so she hurriedly put on her crew cap and headset.

"Oh, but why were we talking about this again?"

"Hmm? Oh, right!" Akiko, almost done dressing, clapped her hands. "So I'm pretty sure one of your friends is in the dining room, Saemi."

"Huh? One of my friends?"

"Yeah, a girl. I think I've seen her a few times before. She's got that classic young-lady business suit on, so I thought maybe she's a friend from a previous job."

That would describe exactly one person in Emi's life.

"...Hey, Emi."

"Oh, it *is* you, Rika! What brings you here?"

The sight of Rika Suzuki, looking a bit abashed as she sipped a large coffee in a corner of the first floor, made Emi smile as she walked up.

"Are you off work?" she asked.

"Y-yeah. I got off a little bit early today, so, um, I was free this evening, so I thought I'd stop on by to see you."

"Oh, really? Well, I'm sorry, but I'm still on for a while. Till ten tonight sadly..."

"I know. I asked."

"Huh? Oh, you did?"

Emi wondered who told her. Just like Chiho, Rika was fully clued in on the situation surrounding Emi, Maou, and Ente Isla. She had been in more frequent contact with Chiho and Suzuno as of late; one of them must have provided the info. Either way, though, why would she come here when she knew Emi still had four hours of work left?

"Ah, I'm sorry," Rika hurriedly added, perhaps picking up on Emi's internal pondering. "I knew you were working late, but, um, I couldn't help myself, or—like—I figured seeing you would help me chill out a little."

"...Is something wrong or—?"

Even Emi could tell something was amiss by now. Rika was talking a mile a minute, she kept staring into space before turning her eyes back toward Emi, and she kept nervously squirming around in her seat. It made Emi recall a time not long ago when she similarly lost her cool.

"Well, um, you don't have work early tomorrow, do you, Emi?"

"No."

"Okay. I can wait, or like, if I'm distracting you, I can kill some time somewhere else first."

"No, no, not distracting..."

"Okay, so, uh, you mind if we chat a bit after you're done tonight? Dinner's on me."

"Well, of course, but what's up? Seriously."

"Ahhhhhhh...I'll tell you later."

It was rare to see Rika act this indecisively.

"You really *are* gonna distract me if I don't know, Rika! If you need some advice, I could spend my shift thinking about the issue until I get off."

"Hmmm, you think? Because it's nothing *that* big, really..."

This was completely impossible. She was acting hideously unnatural.

"But okay, so, um..."

"Yeah?"

After all her previous hesitation, it still took Rika two or three more deep breaths to gain the will to continue.

"So earlier...Ashiya called to ask me out..."

"........Oh................................ Oh, okay."

Emi could hear her own voice from some corner of her mind reminding her that *this* was what happened last time, too. She did indeed have trouble focusing for the rest of her shift.

THE HERO
ATTEMPTS TO
WRANGLE THE
UNWRANGLEABLE

"Hello, Bell? Sorry to call you so late. I know this is sudden, but do you think I could stay at your place tonight? ...Yeah, I just finished up work, but something came up... Rika came to my MgRonald. She's got something important to talk about, and we're not planning to be *that* late, but I'm not sure I'll make the last train."

"Very well. Please give Rika my regards. Hngh!!"

"Huh? ...Okay, um, thanks. I'll send a text or something when I'm coming back, okay?"

"Right. I think I will likely be up late tonight as well, so there is no need to... Curse you!! *Feel free to contact me whenever you think you are...* Shut up! *Ready to come here."*

"A-all right. Thanks..."

Things certainly sounded boisterous on the other end. Besides Suzuno's voice, there was also a mixture of shouting and jeering. It didn't seem to be her late arrival that bothered Suzuno, but the dull, rhythmic thudding in the background that served as a kind of background music to the whole call also gave Emi pause.

"Ah, yes. Laila is waiting at her apartment. She has something she wishes to discuss with you."

"What?"

Emi winced. But it was nothing she could complain at Suzuno about.

"Concerning something wholly different from the request she had of you before, it seems."

"You didn't ask what it was?"

"I did find out, yes... Just keep quiet, *you! I am on the phone, so knock it off!!"*

"Bell?"

By the sounds of things, someone was in the room with Suzuno. And if *this* was the way Suzuno was addressing them, it couldn't have been anyone but her three demonic neighbors.

"Are you busy right now, maybe?"

"In a way, yes, but no worries. I have control over the situation. Alas Ramus is on my side as well."

What could be going on? Emi had trouble even imagining.

"Anyway, I did find out, but I think it best that you hear it directly from the mouth of Laila, Emilia, so I will refrain from telling you. She said she will wait as long as necessary, so feel free to visit her ahead of me. She should be awaiting you in Nord's room."

"...Okay."

"Farewell, then... All right, if you have an excuse, I would like to hear it!"

It was with that ill-boding statement that Suzuno chose to end the call.

"What was that all about...?"

Judging by the clues, it seemed most likely that Maou had done something to invite Suzuno's ire upon him. But what did "Alas Ramus is on my side" mean? The sight of Alas Ramus abandoning him would hurt Maou far more than any physical blow Suzuno had to offer.

"...Ah, well. Before that..."

Emi used her phone to tell Emeralda, still shacking up at her apartment in Eifukucho, that she'd be staying with Suzuno tonight. After receiving her acknowledgment, she let out a sharp exhale.

"Right. *This* is what I should focus on!"

Rika wound up waiting in the dining hall all the way until Emi's shift ended. It wasn't the first time she had gone to her for Ashiya-related advice. However, something was much different this time: Rika knew all about Ashiya's real identity. She had never seen him in demon form, as the Great Demon General Alciel, but she knew both his history and what goals he had in mind as he lived out his daily grind.

Even so:

"Ashiya called to ask me out..."

Which meant—

"...................What should I even do? Ugggh."

She looked at the clock. It was already fifteen minutes past ten. It'd be mean to make Rika wait much longer, and stewing here in the staff room would just get her home later and make her more of a thorn in Suzuno's side.

"Guess I'll have to see how this flows."

Her resolve firmed up, Emilia marched resolutely out of the room, said her good-byes to Akiko and the rest of the crew, and left the building with Rika.

"I'm sorry this is so sudden."

Rika followed behind Emi, her body looking a measure smaller than usual.

"Oh, it's fine. Sorry I made you wait so long. I know we were talking about dinner, but you ate a pretty decent amount, didn't you, Rika?"

"Yeah, I guess, but whatever you want to have, Emi!"

"It'll probably have to be a bar at this point, I'd imagine."

"A bar...? You okay with that?"

"Why wouldn't I be? We've been to lots."

"Yeah, but you aren't actually twenty yet, are you?"

"Oh, thaaaat."

Emi's actual chronological age hadn't reached twenty—when Japanese people could legally drink. This apparently bothered Rika's conscience.

"There was no real regulation on that where I'm from, and I'm pretty sure I'm twenty-one by now as far as my Japan registry goes, so I'm fine along those lines. But would you prefer to talk about this sober?"

"N-no, no, not that. I'm just not sure I can really keep my cool right now, so..."

She hadn't been keeping it for a long time now, but Emi nodded anyway. Alcohol right now, she reasoned, would make Rika ramble her way to oblivion without getting anywhere.

"There's a diner down this road a little bit. Does that work?"

"Sure. Sorry."

Rika was nothing but apologies tonight.

"It's all right. But...you know, you don't have to treat me. Depending on how this goes, Rika, I might have to drop some truth bombs on you that you won't like. Let's have dinner like normal."

"...Okay."

Their destination settled, Emi and Rika trudged their way to the diner, their legs feeling heavier than usual. It was past ten thirty now, and the diner was more empty than not. Taking a nonsmoking booth, they gave their orders—Rika opting for the free-refills drink bar, Emi attacking her post-shift hunger with the clams vongole pasta set with soup, salad, and drink.

"Kinda feels like a while since it was just you and I eating together, huh?"

"Yeah. Too bad we aren't taking the same route back home any longer. I'm glad you're willing to come here all the time to see me, but I still feel kinda bad about it."

"Oh, don't worry about it! I mean, regardless of the circumstances, you'd feel kinda weird hanging around the office you got fired from, right?"

"I don't think it's *that* bad. I mean, all the restaurants and stuff you took me to around that office really helped me get used to Japanese cuisine, Rika. I'll travel to you next time, so how 'bout we invite Maki and so on if we're all free?"

"Yeah, the scene keeps changing all the time over there! Remember that Russian place we all kept going to? That closed down last month."

"Aw, no way! I really loved the beef stroganoff there."

"Yeah, they kept all the furniture and opened up this pasta joint there, but it just wasn't any good. Like, with all the Italian and stuff in the area, you can't afford to disappoint with the food like that. There were a lot of the old fixtures and stuff in the place, too, so it felt sad."

"Yeah, with all that fancy Russian stuff they had on the walls, it'd be weird if they opened a ramen or rice bowl joint in there."

"Well, it's never a problem if the food's good. Too bad the good places can't all stay open like that, y'know?"

As they darted from one light subject to the next, the (coincidentally) pasta dinner set arrived.

"Wow, looking at that makes me kinda hungry now."

"Why don't you get something?"

"Mmm, I didn't really do much exercise today, so I dunno if I want anything heavy...hmm..."

Rika agonized over the subject for a few more minutes before deciding against it. Emi was done with her meal not long after, and Rika took the cue to pour herself a cup of herbal tea from the drink bar, mentally prepping herself. She turned toward Emi in the booth, straightening up her posture.

"So..."

"Yeah?"

Emi nodded at her as she took a swig of water.

"I think I called you about pretty much the same thing a while ago, Emi, but... You know, this time, Ashiya called me to ask for help purchasing a cell phone."

"Wow, so he's using you as his personal electronics consultant again?"

Back when Maou had purchased a TV, Ashiya had mentioned to Rika that he was considering a phone purchase of his own, asking for her advice. He wound up not buying one that day, and with the multiple waves of drama to deal with afterward, Ashiya still didn't have a mobile phone to his name.

"That's the general idea," Rika said, choosing not to deny it. "But he said he wanted to apologize for all the stuff that happened and for not telling me about everything. So he asked me out to dinner."

"Bfft!!"

The instinctual muscular reaction from Emi almost made her crush the glass of water in her clenched hand.

"T-to *dinner*?!"

It was a standard tactic to use whenever a man asked a woman out. But if the man and woman were Ashiya and Rika, that changed things.

"S-so then?"

"I had no reason to turn him down, so I said okay. Probably a little *too* eagerly."

Emi had no way of knowing where this eager approval was made, but she could tell that Rika was ready, willing, and able to accept the invite the moment she received it.

"Oh..."

She paused for a moment, embarrassed. Then she imagined the two of them having dinner out. It made her want to cradle her head with both hands. This was *Ashiya* she was talking about. Ashiya who (for reasons different from most others) had no motivation whatsoever to dress gaudily or brag about himself with others. If this was Maou, there *would* be some of that bragging. He'd probably be inspired to take her to kind of a nicer restaurant. Emi had seen him engage in this kind of date scene once before, and while it wasn't until later when she learned Ashiya had coordinated his outfit for him, between that and his work attitude, she had learned early on that Maou could hold himself pretty well during more formal occasions.

Meanwhile, flip that over, and you had Ashiya. He had a clean-cut image and took good care of his looks, but unlike with Maou, Emi had no recollection of him wearing anything memorable at all in public. The more she tried to recall some occasion—any occasion—the more she just remembered him in shorts during the summer or T-shirts while out handling chores. With each memory, less and less of his body was covered.

"S-so where will you be eating?"

"I dunno, but I think I understand your worries there, Emi." Rika let out a wry smile at her clearly disturbed friend. "I know how Maou and his friends live. If we wind up at Manmaru Udon for noodles or MgRonald even, I'm not gonna complain."

"I think you probably *should*, actually."

If that was what Rika was willing to accept, Emi wasn't sure what advice she could offer.

"But that's not what you wanted to talk about, right?"

"Well, no point asking *you* what Ashiya eats, yeah?"

"Yeah."

"I mean, you told me you might have some truth bombs, but... Yeah. That sort of thing."

"What sort of thing?"

"I mean, what I want to talk about… Basically, I'm afraid it's gonna be a rehash of all the stuff I already know from you and Maou and stuff. I think it's just gonna be Ashiya personally apologizing to me, in terms of what he wants to say to me, I mean. Like, he told me that already."

"Yeah…"

Emi hadn't had much to contribute besides "yeah" for much of this conversation.

"So, you know…"

Now Rika was starting to get fidgety again.

"I'm thinking I should take this chance to really blow it all up."

"Huh? Blow what up?"

"Um, you know, the, uhh…"

"Yeah?"

Rika's face was growing redder by the moment. She squirmed, barely able to piece together the words as her breathing grew ragged.

"I—I, you know, like, to be honest. I, um, I think I—I really like Ashiya and stuff, so…"

"I know. So?"

"…………Huh?"

"Huh?"

"…Um, why?"

"Why what?"

"Huh?"

The reddened Rika and the deadly serious Emi locked eyes silently for a moment.

"You…know? Like, *what*?"

"Are you surprised that I knew, Rika?"

"…Yeah. Like, I mean, I—when I said that—I thought I was gonna, um, die of embarrassment, but I held out, so…"

That might have been the case, but as mean as it was to Rika, it was already incredibly old news to her friend.

"Well, I'm sorry, Rika, but…probably, if anyone saw you and Alciel and how you acted, there's no way they wouldn't notice."

"…You think so?"

"Probably."

"What about, um, Ashiya…?"

"Him I wouldn't be so sure about…but I have a hunch, and the Devil King and Bell have picked up on it."

Rika blinked for a few moments.

"Maou and Suzuno……… Gahh?!"

"Rika?!"

The sudden shriek was accompanied by Rika's forehead falling onto the table so hard their glasses were virtually thrown into the air.

"Oh *noooooooooooooooooo*! How could I have forgotten?! He totally *said* so on that daaaaaaay!!"

"Wh-whoa, keep it down, Rika! What're you talking about all of a sudden?"

"Aaaaaaahhhhhhhhhh, he told me he knew… I knew it, ngghhh, Maou, on that daaaaay…"

"The Devil King? What did he say to you? You mean on that day when he bought the TV?"

"Yesssssss! That day!! Maou— Maou said to me, he noticed what I feel, *aaaahhhhh*!!"

This fresh young maiden, so hesitant to lay out her true feelings only a moment ago, was now groaning and carrying on like a Malebranche tribesman whose claws had been torn off.

"He said, 'Did you fall for Ashiya?' Like, just like that! Maou did! Maou totally said it, that bum! He told me! *Aaaahhh!* And then Suzuno punched him out and started choking him! What the hell? What the hell?! I'm, like…! Why did I have to carry on like such an idiot around them, all over Ashiya?! I'm so ashamed, I'm so ashamed, I'm so ashamed I could die, why does life have to be so embarrrrrassinnnng?!"

"…Devil King…!"

She had no idea what the context of this conversation was, but Emi would be sure to thoroughly interrogate Maou about it within the next few days.

"It's all right. It's all right, Rika. The Devil King may not be too delicate a lot of the time, but he's not the kind of guy to just spout that stuff with no prompting, and I'm pretty sure it never would've made it to Alciel…to Ashiya, I mean."

GRAND MEN

"You *thiiiiink*? Because I really think it would've by now!!"

Rika lifted her head. The tip of her nose was now bright red, tears welling up in her eyes.

"L-look, it's fine, all right? It's fine. Bell throttled him that same day, so worst-case scenario, the rumor mill stopped right there..."

"Emiiiii, am I imagining things, because it sure doesn't *sound* like you're very confident about thaaaaaat?!"

"...Sorry. I can't give you an absolute guarantee."

"Aaaaaaaaaaaaaaaaaaaaaaaaaaaaaahh!"

She couldn't lie to Rika. So instead, Emi gave her honest opinion.

"B-but Ashiya asked you out himself, didn't he? And he didn't act awkward or anything when he did, right? I'm sure it's fine. Let's be optimistic about this!"

"Um, yeah, he sounded the same as always over the phone, but *ahhh*, I'm nervous, I'm so nervous all of a sudden! Ashiya used to be this really brainy war general, yeah? Like, strategizing behind the scenes so nobody would notice? That kind of thiiiiiiiiiing!!"

"N-no, it's fine, it's fine! You'd be really surprised how emotional he can be. He can't hide anything like that!"

The main emotional moments for Ashiya were limited to when someone insulted Maou, or Urushihara embezzled his funds, or finances grew tighter, or an unexpected expense popped up, but that was really the only thing Emi could tell her.

"S-so what did you want advice about, Rika?! If you want to learn more about Alciel, then I'm sorry, but I don't think I can tell you any more than what we did before!"

"Nnnnhh..."

Rika looked up at Emi, still teary-eyed. That look didn't change the facts. Emi had nothing else to say. Whether as Shirou Ashiya or as the Great Demon General Alciel, Emi had only so much personal information she could relate about him. Even considering the grudges of the past, he was a sincere, unaffected, and extremely frugal person, walking around in clothing selected with cost performance first in mind and not being at all picky with what he ate. He wasn't as obsessed as Maou about obtaining certifications and so on, but all the time spent at the library gave him a fairly broad knowledge of the world, and he would occasionally exhibit some bizarrely humanlike talents to keep the Devil's Castle from falling in the red.

But Emi had mostly heard secondhand about all this. She hadn't witnessed it for herself. His cooking talents *were* first-rate by homemade standards, one of the few abilities that Emi had to admit defeat with. His skills with electronics were sparse—he didn't own any and never had the chance to use them—but he had already asked Rika for phone advice, so she'd come into this knowing that.

"So what I can say to you really isn't all that different from what I gave you before. I don't know how much I can help you with this date, honestly..."

"Don't call it a date! You're embarrassing me! I don't think *he* thinks of it as a date!"

"What else do you want me to call it?"

"I—I don't know, but... Arrgh, why do I have to embarrass myself so *bad* like this?!"

That's what Emi wanted to know.

Rika bounced around on her padded booth seat for a bit longer, her breathing uncontrolled and face bright red.

"The...the advice I want... Ugh, I'm so embarrassed; it's so hot in here, my heart hurts... I really want to ask you, Emi! ...I..."

The moment Rika tried her hardest to spit it out, Emi's mind gave her a new vision. She had seen this sort of expression before, these sorts of feelings.

"I—I want to know whether it's...it's okay for me to like Ashiya!"

"..."

I knew it, she thought as she nodded.

"I don't really know what to say to that."

"Oh. c'mon!" Rika craned her neck forward. "Like, I couldn't ask anyone besides you, Emi!"

"Why's that?"

"Why? Um... I mean, because Ashiya's..."

Emi couldn't help but smile as she watched Rika try to defend herself.

"Because Ashiya's friends with the demon who destroyed my homeland? What's that got to do with you, Rika?"

"Ah…"

Rika half rose to her feet. The two of them exchanged glances, one higher than the other.

"…Nothing?"

"Is what I think," Emi said as she looked up at her.

"Really?"

"Yeah."

Rika gasped. "…Why?"

"It's a road we've already gone down a long time ago."

"Already gone down?"

"Yeah." Emi calmly took another sip from the water glass she nearly crushed earlier. "I mean, it's kind of gone beyond familiar with our interactions these days, but the fact is that me and Alciel are still enemies."

"Right, so…"

"But I can't just take away the feelings you have for him, Rika."

Having her own feelings recited back to her point-blank made the temperature of Rika's face rise a little once more.

"You still have those kinds of feelings, too, even after knowing about our past, and you're worried about that, aren't you?"

"Um, well, yeah. You and Suzuno and Emeralda. All you Ente Islans."

Rika failed to notice Emi's use of the word *too.*

"Right. But that still doesn't matter. Of course…"

Emi recalled images of Rika in her mind, along with another vital friend of hers.

"I'm not exactly gonna be cheering from the sidelines, and if Alciel tries anything dangerous, I'm gonna put public safety way above your own feelings, Rika. But ultimately, it's our fault he's in Japan right now, and you met him and started having a thing for him without knowing any of that. Do you think I have any right to meddle with that?"

They had just finished up a meal the last time Emi dealt with this, too, hadn't they? Emi recalled how large and round *that* girl's eyes were, at the end of that.

"So I want you to keep deciding on your own feelings, Rika."

"……Yeah." Rika finally settled back into her seat, giving Emi a blank stare. "And here I thought you'd tell me to think about how people on Ente Isla feel, or about how I didn't know anything about the war, or whatever."

"I won't talk about that, no, but in a way, what I'm telling you is a lot tougher than that. I mean…"

"I know, I know. You're telling me you might kill this guy I like without mercy, if you have to."

"Right." Emi nodded with a grin. "That's one rule I'm never compromising on. Not that it means very much right now."

"Oh?"

"Like, I really can't imagine any of them exposing anybody in Japan to danger at this point. As long as they're in Japan, there's absolutely no way I could kill them. I *used* to have my dead father to blame them for, so I could use my grudge about that to draw the line with them, but not now."

"Oh…yeah." Rika let out a soft sigh. "So what do you think about them all now? Maou and Ashiya and Urushihara."

"…They're my enemies."

The reply came after a short period of reflection. The point wasn't lost on Rika, and Emi herself was fully aware of it.

"My father was alive the whole time, but what the demons did completely wrecked the path of my life, changing it from what it should've been…or what I *think* it should've been, at least. That's as true now as it was then. And there are all these people that died full of regrets thanks to them. All this sadness from the relatives and friends they left behind. I still need to make them take that in, from my heart. The just deserts I haven't delivered yet."

But that simply wasn't enough, by now, to fan the flames of hatred within Emi. This, too, she was fully aware of.

"I've thought about it time and again. There's no point obsessing about theoreticals, but even if the Devil King didn't do anything, Ente Isla was in a constant state of war between its nations. And there's always war somewhere on Earth, too, isn't there? Japan's relatively peaceful, but people are dying on a daily basis in conflicts big and small worldwide. It just so happened that I was confronting the

Devil King, and I had the power to face off against him. I was nearly killed countless times, and you know, seeing girls my age in Japan who live these carefree lives and don't have to fear potentially dying tomorrow...I'm jealous of that. But no matter how jealous I am, I can't alter my past to be more like theirs."

Emi clutched Rika's hand above the table.

"Plus, I don't want to think that making friends with you, and the time I spent here, is thanks to my life being wrecked. If I could live my life all over again, I don't want to pick one for myself where I didn't meet you."

"Emi..." Rika looked at her hand, her cheeks reddening again. "I-I'm glad you think so much of me like that, but I'm really no one that amazing..."

"The only person who can decide how valuable you are to me is me, Rika. And you're a valued friend. Someone I can't cut out from my life."

The words came straight and true to the utterly confused Rika.

"Nnh... Now—now I'm getting all embarrassed for totally different reasons, girl! You keep buttering me up like that, you'll make Emeralda all jealous next."

"Yeah. But the difference is that Eme is somebody way high up in society. Someone I'd normally never get to talk with. Being able to chat and laugh with someone like that is one achievement I've made in my life. She may not look it, but you won't find a more reliable woman out there."

"I'm sorry if this is rude, but I still can't believe she's older than you, Emi."

"Do I look that much older than her? Wow. I remember Chiho being all surprised about my age, too, long ago."

"Well, Emeralda looks like a little girl, and not to put it *this* way, but maybe it's the hard life you've led that makes you mature beyond your age, Emi. You don't feel younger than me at all, and maybe you act more your age when it's all informal like this, but from the side, I mean, you look as grown-up as that manager at Maggie's."

"If I remind you of Ms. Kisaki, *that* sure makes me proud as a woman, yeah..."

Emi smiled and removed her hand from Rika's.

"But getting back to the topic, there's really no need for you to worry about me, Rika. Just go where your feelings take you."

"Oh, yeah, we *were* talking about that, weren't we? But you know, I'm dealing with you right now. Once I'm right in front of him, I might wind up ducking out before I can even do anything."

"If it happens, it happens. That's another choice available to you, Rika. There's nothing rare about it—wanting to confess your love but failing to in the end."

"Ugh, stop it! This is *soooo* embarrassing!"

Rika started squirming yet again, hands against her face.

"I know I shouldn't bring this up yet again, but I'm amazed you can cut through all the crap like that. Even though these are your sworn enemies I'm talking about..."

"I told you, we're past that road."

She certainly sounded emboldened, enough even to surprise herself. But Emi's thoughts about back then were now fully solidified in her mind. Maou, Ashiya, and Urushihara were enemies of mankind on Ente Isla, but none of that had anything to do with Japan or even Earth. They had every right to be loved on Earth, and if needed, she wouldn't hesitate to take their lives precisely *because* they were no longer related.

"When you say that, are you talking about Chiho?"

"In some ways, Chiho's stronger than any of us right now, but she's still only about as mature as her current age. She learned about the Devil King and me strictly solo, nobody to talk to or be protected by. It must have been hellish to deal with."

"Yeah, talk about shocking. Like, didn't you break your leg or something back when Urushihara was fighting Maou and you saved her from getting crushed by highway debris?"

Rika was recalling what Chiho herself had told her while Emi was incommunicado in Ente Isla.

"Pretty much, yeah. No joke, it was like she was thrown into a summer blockbuster film all by herself, and nobody on Earth has any memory of it besides her. I couldn't imagine how scary it was."

"Any memory? What do you mean?"

Emi pointed at her own temple as a quizzical Rika stared at her. "I suppose you could call it memory control? Me, Bell, and the Devil King are able to rewrite people's memories to some extent."

Rika opened her eyes wide. "Really? With your magic or whatever?"

"It's two different things, actually. The Devil King uses demonic force; we use holy force. But the effect on the target's the same, I suppose. And *you* haven't heard about the Shuto Expressway falling to pieces, right? Like, people would be talking about that for five, ten years after the fact. But the Devil King put up a barrier to keep anyone on the outside from watching, and then he erased the memories of everyone inside for only a few short moments. Which makes it sound easy, I guess, but you'd need to be a Devil King to pull that off. For us and Suzuno, it takes a lot of effort just to erase one person's recollections."

"Wow, this sounds like something really freaky I'm hearing..."

"I know I lied to you about where I was from, Rika, but I swear to you that I've never done anything to your memories."

"Ooh, yeah. I remember Maou saying he could erase all the scary ones when we first started talking about Ente Isla. There were all these crazy revelations at the time, I was like *Come on, can you really?* But if you think about it, yeah, pretty frightening. There aren't any criminals or whatever on Ente Isla that take advantage of that?"

"Hmm, I don't know. I heard there was a sort of antidote magic that could restore memories, so I don't think the holy-magic approach totally eliminates them. I only studied the fundamentals so I don't know for sure, but Bell probably would..."

"Ah, that's fine; not like me knowing about *that* in detail would help me much. It does seem kinda weird, though..."

Rika had picked up on something. Emi knew what it was but asked anyway.

"What's weird?"

"Like why Maou didn't erase any of Chiho's memories with all the rest of them."

"...Yeah."

Emi nodded deeply.

"Maou treats Chiho as really, really precious, I'd say. But...not to be mean. I wasn't hurt or anything, but after that Gabriel guy freaked me out and I came down with a fever and all that... I mean, hey, that was a lot of trauma! And she nearly *died*, too. I don't know how any normal person can overcome that kinda fear..."

"Yeah. And she's seen all of them in full demon form, too."

"By 'demon form,' do you mean how Maou and them all look normally? Um... I haven't seen that yet, but were they, like, whoa, real *monsters*? Like I'm picturing them?"

"It depends on how you define *monster*, but if you're asking me whether a normal high school girl would want to hang out with one, I'd have to say it would be pretty unlikely. Did you want more details?"

"...For future reference maybe."

Now Rika nodded, her face more severe. She must have been concerned about what her potential love looked like.

"I'd say Lucifer, or Urushihara, has the least difference between his two forms. The only big one is the large black wings. Otherwise, he looks like he does now."

"Oh, they don't change too much?"

"Well, as the demon Alciel, Ashiya has two scorpion-style tails."

"T-tails?!"

Technically speaking, it was a single forked tail. Emi, who wasn't *that* much of an expert on the rear ends of demons, simply relayed her understanding of it to Rika.

"His skin's really tough, like the shell of a lobster, but made out of metal that swords can't cut through. That covers everything from his face to his arms and the rest of his body. His natural voice is incredibly grating to the ears. You could describe his overall shape as human if you squinted hard enough, but he's a little taller than how you know him. In terms of the parts he had clothes over, like his feet, I haven't really seen those in detail, either, so I couldn't tell you."

"A—a lobster...?"

Rika's imagination was failing her mightily. All she could imagine was the spiny lobsters that take center stage in a traditional Japanese

New Year's meal, dancing in and out of her mind, with Ashiya's head on top of them.

"That's...kind of hard to picture..."

"Yeah, well, in terms of looking human, the Devil King's a good deal closer than that."

"Oh, really?"

"Yeah, but he's almost ten feet tall, his arms and legs are the size of tree trunks, he's got horns and hooves on his feet, and there's also these wings he can take out or remove anytime he wants."

Calling this closer to human was a bit of a stretch. It made the look on Rika's face even blanker.

"What do you mean, 'take out or remove'?"

"I don't know. Maybe that's his actual body, maybe it's demonic magic at work. He can still fly without those wings, though, so I'm not exactly sure what they're for."

"You aren't embellishing this, are you?"

"How would I even do that?"

Emi could understand why Rika would doubt her, having never seen these demons in person. But it was all the truth.

"Whew... I just can't imagine them at all."

"I doubt they'll be kind enough to show you if you ask, and it might even kill you unless we take some precautions, so we might have to disappoint you."

"Huh? Why would I die?"

"Being exposed to high levels of demonic force is potentially lethal to normal human beings. These are all upper-class demons so they can take measures to prevent too much force from leaking out, but we can't guarantee that there won't be any aftereffects."

"......"

Now it was Rika tensing her face.

"But you're fine right now, though. Even without any demonic force, they can live off food like anyone else, and I get the impression Ashiya's deliberately removed the force from his own body, so it won't be dangerous to hang out near him."

"You're making him sound like some poisonous spider..."

"In terms of handling, it might be pretty close to that."

Emi's voice grew a bit louder. The more honestly she talked about these demons, the more it resulted in her slamming the man her friend loved.

"Man, talk about a thorny path to tread. Beyond thorny."

"Yeah," Emi agreed.

"But I guess someone else went down that path before me, huh?"

"Yeah. And if that girl was born in Ente Isla, I bet she would've been one hell of a celebrity."

"She already is, in my book. Like, before I came along, she was the only one who had this huge secret she knew? No way I could handle that stress."

"Yeah… You're right."

Like Chiho, Rika came to know the truth about Emi only after Ente Isla–related events put her in mortal danger. But there was a marked difference in how they were treated after the big reveal. Rika was attacked by Gabriel and the knights of Ente Isla's Eastern Island, sent there to kidnap Ashiya, and was rescued by Amane Ohguro's intervention. As she put it, she had come down with a fever subsequently, Chiho coming to take care of her and later guiding Maou, Suzuno, Urushihara, and Amane to provide further treatment.

What about Chiho, however? Suzuno and Amane weren't on the scene back then, and Emi and Ashiya weren't close acquaintances yet. Lucifer and Olba had kidnapped her, she had been caught up in a crazy, out-of-this-world battle, and then she was faced with this guy at work she liked being the demon lord of another planet. There was nobody to share her memories with once it all wrapped up. It was easy to imagine the pain she must've felt, between her feelings of affection and her recollection of the fight. Despite all the revelations after becoming full, secret-free friends with Emi, it took a fair amount of time for her to be able to talk normally with Maou again.

"Chiho acts totally unaffected, but I know she's suffered a lot. Or maybe *is* suffering, in fact."

She knew about Maou and his true form. Her life had been threatened multiple times. Now they were setting foot upon a new truth once more, but no matter how it worked out, Emi doubted it would do much to change Chiho's feelings.

"Can I ask kind of a blunt question?"

"What?" Emi asked, eyebrow raised as Rika gave her a grim look.

"Your father married an angel, right?"

"...Right."

Emi's hesitation stemmed from her still-vibrant resistance toward calling Laila her "mother" with her own tongue. Rika paid it no mind.

"So have any people ever...been together with demons before?"

This *was* a blunt question. But it was one that would naturally occur to anyone who knew about Emi's parents. And the answer Emi had was clear as day.

"I don't know of any."

It was literally a case of devil's advocate. If people and angels could share a relationship like that, then why not people and demons?

"...No, not like I'd know at this point anyway."

Rika gave this a soft smile and a nod.

"Thanks, Emi. I appreciate you staying up this late to listen to me."

She looked up. The clock on the wall was nearing midnight.

"No, it's been really fun, sharing a meal with you for a change. Can you catch a train back home?"

"Yeah, I checked beforehand. I've still got enough time, but don't you have Alas Ramus with Suzuno right now, Emi? You don't want to be *too* late, for their sakes, I don't think."

"I warned them in advance...but thanks for thinking about them. I forgot to ask this whole time, but when's the big day?"

"Tomorrow afternoon."

"That's kind of fast."

"I know, but tomorrow was pretty much the only free day both of us had for the time being." Rika flashed a bashful smile. "That's why I came to you in such a big huff, too, hee-hee-hee."

"Ohh. Well, I know I said I can't cheer you on, but still, good luck out there."

"Yeah. Honestly, right now, I don't really know what's the best-case scenario I should even be gunning for."

Rika stood up, reaching for the bill as she prepared to leave. Emi stopped her. "No," she said, "lemme pay for what I ate."

"Oh, I can't let you do that!"

"I can't let *you* do that. If you go back long enough, I'm the one who oughta be buying you a meal anyway. So let's just split it today, like always."

"...No defying you, I guess."

Emi's emphasis on doing it "like always" made Rika raise her hands in defeat.

After splitting away from Rika at Hatagaya station, Emi headed down the path toward Villa Rosa Sasazuka alone.

In her heart of hearts, she saw little chance of Rika's feelings fully coming across to Ashiya. Her impression of him was that, unlike Maou, he always made an effort to keep a prudent distance from the people he dealt with. He never fully dove into the human being role the way Maou did, didn't adjust himself to human society the way Maou did—but didn't act needlessly hostile toward them, either, like he used to.

"But if it *does* turn out okay despite that, it'd sure surprise me..."

Emi watched her breath dissipate into the streetlights as she quickened her pace a little. She had people waiting for her at Villa Rosa. True friends, people she loved wholeheartedly, in the apartment where her sworn enemy lurked.

It had been a little over a month since she became a regular there, even sharing a workplace with friend and foe. It was hopelessly complex, ever changing, and—as Emi thought to herself amid the light from the telephone poles, cars, and convenience stores that leaked out from all around her—so unbelievably comfortable for her that she wished it could continue forever.

She was well used to this path, and the light from the apartments already loomed ahead. Two of them were still on upstairs; Maou and Suzuno must have still been up. The sight of those lights gave comfort to her heart, something that began happening somewhere in the past.

"Oh, man. None of this should be happening, but here we are..."

After everything she just told Rika, too. Her mind must be crashing with some kind of error again.

"...Hmm?"

Then she wondered if her eyes were failing her as well. Something odd was in sight up there—someone kneeling primly in the corridor. Two of them. It made Emi instinctively hide herself behind the wall surrounding the site.

"Emi finished her shift ages ago. Where the hell is she?"

"Bell said she had to meet up with a friend after that..."

It was Maou and Laila. For reasons only they knew, they were braving the cold out there, curled up and shivering.

"A friend? Rika Suzuki?"

"I don't know who, but she said the person showed up at her workplace out of nowhere..."

"Definitely Rika, then. She visits the MgRonald all the time."

"I don't know that name. She's friends with Emilia?"

"Yeah. She's from Earth, but she knows all about who we are. I guess she's Emi's best friend, so she probably knows about you, too."

"Oh, really? Well, that's nice. Having a friend you can talk about anything with."

"Yeah, but did this really have to happen *today*? Thanks to Suzuno, I can't go inside until Emi gets back, but if Rika's taking up her time, who knows when she'll be back?"

Laila was presumably there to ambush Emi so they could have that talk Suzuno had warned her about, but Maou's motives were a mystery to her. Their relationship had changed over time, yes, but there's no way the Devil King would let himself freeze to death just to welcome her to his apartment. The phone call earlier indicated to Emi that Suzuno might have been giving him the business (and then some) a bit ago—did that have something to do with it? If Suzuno wanted to boot him out of the apartment, it seemed unlikely Ashiya would be willing to accept that.

But as Emi's thoughts proceeded along those lines—

"I haven't done this in a while, have I?"

She recalled how she used to go on stakeout missions like these to Villa Rosa Sasazuka all the time. The arrival of Alas Ramus allowed her to make regular sanctioned visits instead, but the era before that seemed like eons ago, even though it wasn't.

"Y'know, I really think we're reading too much into this, but…"

"Whether you think so or not, it'll sound like nothing more than a trite excuse to a woman. You were wrong in the end, were you not? No matter how effective the attempt, it's pointless without results."

"Like you're one to talk."

"Look, I'm sorry, but it's true. I've met tons of people from a lot of countries by this point, but it's pretty weird, you know? The way they all get into arguments over the same things."

"We aren't arguing."

"Maybe it'd be better if you were. At least you'd be trying to express yourselves to each other."

"What's that supposed to mean?"

It seemed like a fairly uncommon conversation for a Devil King and archangel to have. It proved to Emi that Maou was out there because he invited a woman's scorn upon him, but who would be enraged enough to drive him to *this*? It wasn't Laila over there, and Emi hadn't seen him all day today. Suzuno sure sounded pissed over the phone, but Ashiya wouldn't put up with this kind of treatment on her part.

Beyond that, the only women who could give Maou this much guff were Amane, Acieth, or the landlord. Perhaps Miki Shiba, the Villa Rosa Sasazuka owner whom Maou and Ashiya found impossible to defy, scolded them to the point that Ashiya reluctantly put his roommate out on the doorstep for the night. That seemed the most likely scenario to Emi. But then the conversation went in a wholly unexpected direction—

"I mean," Laila said with a sigh, "it sounds to me like you're letting her spoil you completely."

"Spoil…? Yeah, maybe, but she should've known this isn't the sort of topic we can really tackle frankly with each other, so…"

There was little force behind Maou's protest. It wasn't the cold fazing him—just the understanding that his attempt at a protest was nothing of the sort at all, but instead something he still felt needed to be said.

"See? 'She should have known.' You let her spoil you that way. And that's led to discontent and distrust in all kinds of situations like this. All over the world."

"Yeahhhhh… But what other way was there to settle this?"

"Whether there's another way or not, did you even try to find one? Did you show any effort like that to her? Or did you just assume that she'd always respect your will and understand your motivations, so you didn't bother showing her a little sincerity?"

"…"

Maou fell silent. Perhaps the words hit home.

"Listen. Maybe that girl really is that incredibly broad-minded and strong inside, but she's still only in high school, all right? She's only had sixteen or seventeen years' experience living in this world. You can't expect her to think the same way as a centuries-old demon like yourself."

"I know that. I know that, but… Ugh, I'm freezing. Why isn't Emi here yet…?"

Emi let out an unconscious gasp. There was only one high school–aged girl who shared a connection with Maou and Laila—and that was Chiho. Did Maou do something to incur her wrath?

"Well, let me just say this. Nobody actually likes bad boys, you know? Not even the ones in movies and TV shows with good looks and lots of money and high social status. They always get their comeuppances in shows like those, and that's because nobody likes them in reality, either."

"Quit talking about TV and movies all the time. Your husband's gonna think you're some kind of degenerate."

"He likes watching samurai dramas, too, so it's fine. And you know how many of those shows have episodes where fancy-pants gigolos go around abusing women? Usually, they don't even make it to the third act. They get killed by the yakuza or some corrupt magistrate first."

"Uh, what were we talking about again?"

"We're talking about how if you hurt the feelings of a beautiful young woman, you'll always have to pay that back with interest."

Emi found much to agree with in Laila's assessment of samurai-drama tropes but quickly snapped out of it.

So Maou had hurt Chiho's feelings somehow. That explained Suzuno's act over the phone and Ashiya's willingness to kick him out of the apartment. Suzuno thought a great deal of Chiho, and she enjoyed at least a measure of respect from Ashiya—treating her far nicer than Urushihara anyway. But the Maou that Emi knew would never do anything to hurt her like that. As she just talked about with Rika, Maou had treated Chiho as someone special in his life for quite a long time. Since joining the MgRonald crew, she knew through discussions with Kisaki and Akiko and Kawata that Maou's public attitude toward her hadn't changed one bit before and after she learned the truth.

"Chiho… Hope she's okay."

Ideally, Emi would've preferred to leave them to shiver out the rest of the night up there and go give Chiho a big hug to console her instead. But it was well past midnight, and storming the Sasaki residence was out of the question. Plus, this was Chiho they were talking about. No matter how cruel Maou was to her, Emi suspected she would never ever bad-mouth him in any way.

But what did Maou *do* anyway? The conversation was lacking much detail so far.

"You are certainly striking a brave stand here, however. Reminds me of me, long ago."

"Ugh, don't give me crap like that. I'll kick your ass down the stairs."

"Ah, I love it when you react like a little boy like that. It's so innocent and… Ahhh?!"

"?!"

The soft shouting from Laila made Emi peek out from behind the wall. She found her there, leaning against the stairway's guardrail in an awkward position, trying to catch her breath. Maou must have quite literally tried to kick her ass down the stairs right then.

"You—you didn't have to actually do it! What if I fell down?!"

"You should be glad an angel like you got away that lightly after taunting the Devil King, man. Plus, you know how many times your daughter took a tumble down those stairs? I just thought I'd let you join in the fun."

The lunacy of Maou's excuses put Laila in a silent state of confusion.

"Did—did you push Emilia down these stairs?"

"No, she slipped and fell by herself. I even caught her fall once, thank you very much."

That *did* happen once, didn't it? Emi had grown far more used to those steep, slippery steps by now, thanks to how many times she was going up and down them these days. Growing more connected to the upstairs landing of Villa Rosa Sasazuka, her fear of that stairway was all but gone now. She let out a sigh from the back of her throat, muffled so Maou and Laila wouldn't notice. It gently ran through her nostrils.

"So what'll you do?"

"...I'm thinking about it."

"Not that it's for me to say, but the longer you leave it unaddressed, the more complicated it's going to become."

"I *really* don't need you telling me that. Will you kiss and make up with your daughter for me already?"

"That's what I'm waiting out here for, remember?"

"Yeah, and let me say, if you're expecting me to thank you for that, you got another think coming. Emi's one of the craziest stubborn people I know. If she doesn't like someone, she's a hell of a lot more ruthless toward them than I am."

"R-really? ...What do you mean, 'ruthless'?"

Emi winced as she detected the slight stiffening in Laila's voice.

"You know, she's had a hard life, so it's not that easy for her to trust in people. Chi or Rika Suzuki are one thing, but—well, you see how close she and Suzuno are. At first, Emi was so suspicious of her, she practically gave up trying to curry her favor."

"...It certainly doesn't seem that way now."

"Not now, no. The only Emi you know is the one you see now and the one you had just given birth to."

"I don't see how that's not true for you!"

"I still got a year or so of a head start. I've wasted a lot of time hanging around her, one way or another."

"...What do you mean, 'wasted'?" Laila balked.

As she listened, Emi scowled, her wrinkles deepening.

"She hates it when things don't turn out fair," Maou continued, "and even if they do, if they don't turn out the way she wants, she gets all emotional about it. She meddles in everything, but she's such a wimp mentally that she freaks out about the dumbest things. I don't know how I deal with her."

Emi was on the other side of the outer wall and couldn't see Maou, but she had no doubt he was closing his eyes tight and frowning as he whined on end. But despite all the verbal abuse he heaped up, none of it irked her in particular.

"What...?"

Instead, there was a slight, passing thought floating in her heart—like a stubborn curry stain on a white handkerchief—that went like this: *Did he really have to go* that *far?*

"Hmm..."

Meanwhile, Laila seemed less than interested in this put-down of her daughter, spouted at her by the enemy of all mankind. That, if anything, sparked Emi's anger. Being her child, things couldn't help but be complicated in her mind. But she held it back, not wanting to accept it.

"Although, granted, I think she's doing a great job taking care of Alas Ramus by herself. She used to go on and on about how I was a bad influence on the kid every time we had a visit, but now she's hangin' out here with her every day she has off, as if that's the new normal for her. Alas Ramus loves it, and I'm sure that's easier for her, too."

"Huh... I see."

"*That's* the only reaction you have? ...Wait, why were we talking about this?"

"We were talking," Laila replied, "about why I can't make up with Emilia that easily."

"Oh, right, right."

He knew that, but it still made Maou lose his momentum and fall silent.

Emi felt it was about time to come out. Having all this bile pointed in her direction made her worry that the curry stain in her heart was going to spread, and she didn't want to admit that to herself. But—

"You know pretty much everything about Emilia, don't you?"

That single statement from Laila glued Emi to her spot once more.

"...Excuse me? What're you talking about?"

"You know her likes, her dislikes, the way she thinks... Almost everything, isn't it? You've clearly been observing her carefully."

"..."

Emi gasped as she felt her cheeks suddenly begin to bake. She sat down on the spot, despite already being hidden from sight, this new reaction throwing her into confusion and fear.

"Why did I...just now...?"

"Man, you really shouldn't say that," Maou retorted. "You're gonna give people the wrong idea."

"Give who the wrong idea? It's only you and me here. I'm just saying, you're obviously taking a lot of consideration for Emilia's feelings. You give her a lot of thought, in your mind."

"Quit talking about that. It was one time."

Maou's voice grew heavier. Maybe he was cupping his head in his hands.

"You don't have to act so ashamed about it."

"I'm not ashamed. I'm watching her because I have to, okay? 'Cause back in the day, Emi was liable to assassinate me in my sleep at any moment. I had to keep tabs on her at all times or else it would've literally been my neck on the line."

"But you *were* watching."

"Would you stop forcing the conversation in that direction?"

"And because you were, you completely failed to notice when Chiho made sure to set up a comfortable, stress-free environment for you."

"........."

"Huh...?"

The unexpected mention of Chiho's name drove Maou to silence and Emi to raise her eyebrows high. Maou wasn't paying enough attention to Chiho?

"Nice of you to clam up when I said that."

"...You're the one who's saying I'm giving excuses, no matter what I really meant."

"I am," Laila replied. Emi could almost hear the grin on her face.

"Even if I was, it wouldn't have been to you. I'll have to make excuses to Ashiya, and Suzuno, and Chi, too, even or else I'll never be let back inside. And why am I kicked out only until Emi gets back here? That makes no sense."

"Maybe because it works out right timewise or maybe for some other reason. There's no way you can visit Chiho's house at this point, either way."

"If I pull anything as crazy as that, it'd make Chi's mom and dad think less of her."

"If you can understand that, why did you miss out on the most obvious thing of all?"

"That's the way I made excuses to you and Suzuno and Ashiya and let her spoil me, isn't it?"

"Maybe."

"Ugghh... Just get here already, Emi... I'm seriously gonna catch a cold otherwise."

The conversation settled to an end at that point. Silence ruled over the apartment building once more.

After all that eavesdropping, it was too clear to Emi that, through some inconsiderate remark or action lodged at Chiho, Maou was kicked out of his apartment until she arrived. That was it, though. That, and Laila's observation that Maou understood Emi more than Chiho—which, if you turned it around, probably hurt Chiho's feelings.

"...I dunno if it was good for me to hear all of that or not."

She began to vaguely understand the situation—and that gave birth to a pure form of panic in her mind. She still didn't have the full picture. Did Maou directly do or say something, or did Chiho react the wrong way to something he unintentionally did?

That was unclear, but one thing wasn't: Chiho was growing jealous of Emi over him.

"Wh-what should I even do...?"

She couldn't even blame Chiho for it. Even with all the furor following Laila showing up and Erone causing all kinds of trouble—even with all the brain errors she used as a convenient excuse—she really had been spoiled by Maou's kindness.

"Wait. I can't jump to conclusions. I need to talk things over with

Bell. And if it's true, then I need to apologize to Chiho about this misunderstanding..."

Before she'd just call it manipulating Maou and remain firm, but now was different. Now she was totally letting Maou spoil her, and she wasn't only allowing it—she had adjusted her heart to the point that she actively *let* him do it. And Chiho picked up on that all too keenly.

"Um, wh-what do you call this? Like, when you're with a criminal for so long, you...some kind of city name, I think...?"

She tried taking her phone out of her bag to look it up. Her hand was shaking, her fingertips too dry to work the screen too well.

"Ah!"

Finally, the phone slipped out of her hand and hit the asphalt below. Maou and Laila didn't seem to notice the dull thud, but now Emi could no longer quiet her trembling heart. If she stayed here, there was no telling what direction her mind would race off toward next. She had a long shift today, and that plus the serious heart-to-heart with Rika had just mentally exhausted her. That's what she had to tell herself, or she wouldn't even be able to stand up any longer.

Groggily, she picked up the smartphone, staggering away from the wall and heading toward the apartment.

"Ah! Emi! God, it's about time you showed up!"

"Huh? Oh, um, Emilia. Uh, welcome back... Ah!"

"Where the hell you think you're walkin'?! Why did you come here from *that* direction?!"

Laila, still too tense and unsure how to deal with Emi to greet her naturally, was pushed aside as Maou rocketed down the stairs.

"...What're you doing up there?" Emi asked in a deliberately reserved voice, ignoring Maou's shouting.

"What was I...? Look, I've been kicked out of my place until you got here, all right? Go see Suzuno for me! I'm gonna die of frostbite in a second! Ashiya! Suzuno! Emi's here! Please let me back in!"

"Ah! Wait...!"

Maou grabbed her by the hand, Unable to shake it off, she found herself pulled upstairs with all his might. She passed by the dumbfounded Laila's face for only a moment before reaching the landing, followed by the wide, curious eyes of Suzuno and Ashiya as they flew out of Rooms 201 and 202. The shivering Maou took the chance to bound back into his apartment.

It was rude of him, undoubtedly, pulling her along without a word of warning. Emi stared blankly into space. She had let him do it, all the way, and she did nothing.

Suzuno flashed an annoyed look at Maou as he fled into his room, then turned toward Emi.

"Alas Ramus is asleep, so keep it quiet. I believe you saw Laila outside. Did you speak with her?"

"Um… Yeah. Hi, Bell. Sorry I didn't text you…"

Emi found it hard to maintain her coherence.

"Mm? Ah. Indeed. Well, if you are done speaking with her, I need to discuss Chiho with you for a moment. I know you must be tired, but I can whip up a fresh batch of tea for us…"

Then Laila chose that moment to stick her neck out from the landing. "Emilia? Um, sorry to keep you after work and everything, but, um, I was waiting for you because I needed to ask you something… I'm sorry, Bell, we haven't spoken yet."

"Oh, you have yet to?"

""We—we had other things,"" mother and daughter responded in unison.

"Mm? What?"

"No, um… What's up with Chiho?"

"Laila takes first priority for now. Please make it quick, Laila."

"All right. So, um, Emilia… Emilia?"

Even as she spoke to Suzuno and Laila, Emi seemed less than completely there with them mentally. It unnerved the angel.

"I'm listening."

"A-all right. Um, so, the day after tomorrow, Satan and Chiho are going to visit my…um, the place I'm keeping in Tokyo. I wanted you to join us."

"Your place? The Devil King and Chiho?"

"R-right. I heard that you, Satan, and Chiho are all off work in the evening two days from now, so, uh, what do you think? Emeralda and Bell could come along, too, if they want."

"Oh…"

…came the halfhearted reply to Laila's fervent plea.

"Alciel and Lucifer don't have any plans, but I don't think they'll be joining us, so…um, I just want to more fully reveal everything that's been vague or unclear up to now, and there are some things I want to give all of you, too, so…"

Ashiya had no plans for two days from now. It wasn't at all the main gist of Laila's plea, but that was about all Emi picked up from it. The very day after the one her best friend, so freely open with her love for Ashiya, planned to put all her chips on the table—even after she had the whole story about him. But Ashiya was staying in his apartment, no particular plans in mind.

Rika's feelings. Chiho's feelings. Her own feelings. She felt like she could see them all, but they remained so elusive at the same time. And no matter how great the life-changing transformations they were going through right now, none of them had much of an effect on the world. Emi felt she was losing herself among this vast chain of emotions, unbroken since ancient times.

And the next thing she knew, she had said—

"Just do what you want. I'm not really interested."

"Ah…"

"Emilia, are you sure?"

The reply shocked Laila into silence and made Suzuno beg for confirmation.

"It's not like going would achieve anything, and it's not like it'll change what you wanna have me do."

"B-but I want you to see, so you can tell I'm acting in good faith. I know I've been putting myself in and out of your lives up to now, but I want to prove all that's over now—"

"If you're ready to do that, then fine. And if the Devil King and Chiho are convinced by it, great. But it's not like me seeing your house will earn anything for me."

"M-maybe not, but…"

"The Devil King's already living like this, and even Sariel and Gabriel aren't far removed from the Japanese mainstream anymore. I'm sure it's the same with you, isn't it? I'm not *that* interested in seeing it for myself. I'm sorry to make you wait in the cold and all that, but I'll pass, thanks. Have a good night."

"E-Emilia!"

"I am sorry, Laila..."

Realizing Emi's mind was made up, Suzuno stepped in front of Laila and invited Emi to join her inside.

Once the shocked-looking angel disappeared from view behind the door, Suzuno settled down next to Emi as the Hero ran a hand through the hair of her daughter, sleeping in a corner of a futon.

"Emilia," she said softly, "are you all right?"

"Was *that* the thing you talked to me over the phone about?"

"Y-yes. Um, the Devil King resisted the idea of visiting Laila's residence before you did, so he made her ask you directly first..."

"Ah. I feel a little bad about making him wait out there, then. After he thought that much about me."

"Hmm?"

The sight of Emi feeling worse for Maou than Laila disturbed Suzuno a bit. But realizing that discussing Laila any further wasn't a smart plan for tonight, she spoke up to change the topic.

"Well, in any case. You saw how the Devil King was kicked out, yes? I asked for him to spend the night outside, but Alciel insisted on compromising, so I reduced it to until you arrived. It all began, you see, when I ran into Chiho in town..."

"The idea of the Devil King putting me above Chiho... That's ridiculous."

"That accursed Devil King was being completely spoiled by Chiho's good intentions, and it drove Chiho to... Pardon?"

"It's not like the Devil King thinks anything of me."

Suzuno's eyes opened wide. "E-Emilia?"

"What did he say? Or was he out with Chiho somewhere?"

"Neither."

"The Devil King, you know," Emi continued, expression calm as she kept patting Alas Ramus's head, "he's kind to everyone he meets. To the point where I'd call him a friend, even though I'm after his life. He's been looking out for me only because I've gone through a lot of trouble and life changes recently. I'm not anything special to him."

"Emilia… Was there something that happened?"

"I'll prove it to you. The Devil King's just as kind to Laila, isn't he? He talks a big game about how much she drives him nuts, but look at how willing he is to wait patiently until she properly takes care of things. He even went through the trouble of coming up with those contract conditions so me and her could make up."

Alas Ramus turned over a bit, away from Emi's hand. It stopped in midair.

"Listen, Bell. The only person the Devil King truly cherishes from the heart…the only one he wants to be with as an equal…is Chiho. What do you think we should do to make Chiho understand that?"

"Th-that…"

Suzuno fell silent.

"It's something the Devil King will have to do, won't he?"

"A-Alciel and I spent much of today lecturing him about that…"

"I'll bet. Because it might look like he treats Chiho as precious, but really it's been the other way around."

"Y-yes. Yes. And then…"

"*He* wants to be treated as precious."

"Oh?"

"…I can't do this tonight. I've had all these complex conversations; my thoughts are gonna get weirder and weirder."

Emi lowered her hand from the air and sighed.

"Maybe I shouldn't say this, Bell, but I've got to tell someone. I hope you'll listen. I need to organize my feelings a little."

"C-certainly," Suzuno said, clearing her thoughts as she stood there.

"Just now, when Laila asked me to visit her place, what do you think my first thought was?"

Suzuno had no reply. Anything she would guess, she surmised, was probably wrong. And that turned out all too correct.

"I thought…well, the Devil King never visited *my* house back when I was his nemesis, Emilia the Hero. So the idea of me visiting Laila's place… Isn't that the most ridiculous bullshit you ever heard of?"

"Emilia…Emilia, you don't really think…?"

"…You know how chaotic my mind is now, right?" Emi raised her exhausted face to Suzuno. "I don't get it. I try to think things over seriously, like *oh yeah, this is it, this is it*, but I know I'm wrong. I'm merely hiding things from myself or trying to explain them away. But I had that thought just now. He never came to *my* place. I really couldn't even consider what he had to say about this. Right now, even being with him would be enough to provoke Chiho. There's no way I could join them the day after tomorrow. If I went there in this state of disarray, I'm worried I'll wind up hearing about everything from Laila. All so I could escape from Chiho and the Devil King... Am I being weird or...?"

"Not...weird, no." Suzuno took a seat next to Emi, lightly caressing her shoulder. "Things have changed far too quickly here for both of us. It takes time to get used to matters."

"Bell...?"

"It takes time," she softly repeated. "Chiho cried because of her feelings toward you. It was the littlest thing that made her unable to contain her jealousy, and it made her so mad at herself and chagrined that she felt that jealousy that it made her cry. We have forgotten that she, too, has experienced vast changes in her life in a short time. That was how strong she seemed to us."

It was true. And neither Emi nor Suzuno had a truly clear idea what was supporting that strength. Chiho was being supported by a firm belief in her heart. That belief alone allowed her to live alongside beings from other worlds who wielded ponderous amounts of power. And it was all so she could remain friends with Emi and Ashiya and Urushihara and Suzuno—so she could continue to share all her feelings, to show affection for what she couldn't share, to keep from being a drag on them all. And that belief was built on the foundation of her feelings for Maou.

"None of us was fully used to this at all. Not in any *real* way. There is still a wall between us and Chiho, in terms of our strength and our worlds, but only Chiho was aware of it. If we want to tear it down..."

"...Only the Devil King can do that. Ugh. This is so messed up."

"And when it *is* torn down, I believe we and Chiho will finally be on the same playing field. The instant it occurs, if Chiho is the only one to have a firm belief like that..."

Suzuno turned her face away from Emi.

"What if it isn't? What if there are other beliefs in play?"

"If there is," Suzuno said with a smile, "then we will become true friends, with no boundaries between us."

Laila, meanwhile, was seated outside, back against the wall of Suzuno's room, head down.

"Emilia..." she half groaned out—and just as she did, the door opened.

"No good?" a worried-looking Nord Justina asked.

"I know"—Laila sighed, her head still down—"that it's not good to panic about this, but...I don't know. What have I been doing with my life all this time? I've lived for millennia, and I have no idea how to make up with my own daughter."

"If anybody knew how parents can find common ground with their children..."

Nord knelt next to his wife, taking her hand and helping her to her feet.

"I'm sure their name would be celebrated for all of history."

The stern-faced father let a slight smile float onto his face as he cheered up his wife.

"We'll have another chance. Look at where we are. You're still alive, and we're reunited here in this peaceful world."

"...Yeah." Laila nodded as they left the upstairs corridor together.

"There's never any telling how our lives will work out. I never expected to be living in a shared space with the Devil King at my age. Compared to that, a mother and daughter fixing their damaged relationship seems much more likely to occur to me."

"And when it happens, you'll be together with us. The three of us as a family."

"You said it... Let's go back home. It's cold out here."

"Say..."

"Hmm?"

The couple looked at each other, halfway down the stairs.

"I really am in a panic right now. I feel like this truly is my last chance. If I let this run through my fingers, I'm not sure I'll be willing to wander like this for another few centuries."

"As long as you and Emilia remain your beautiful selves, I wouldn't mind at all."

"I don't want that! I'm not sick of living, but I want to be a human being. I want Emilia to be one, too. I want to treat each day as special, exactly like all the countless families do as a given here, and I want to die at the end of it. I couldn't imagine anything besides living with you and Emilia."

"...In that case, now is the time for patience." The husband carefully guided his wife down the stairs. "I hope there's something I can do for that...but it's times like these that I hate being just another human. If I could fight to protect you both, at least..."

"You made me human. That's more than enough of a gift."

She gave her husband a peck on the cheek and smiled.

"Thank you, my dear. I'll keep trying tomorrow."

"Great."

"Also..."

"Mmm?"

"Um... Don't be too surprised, all right? About my...place."

"Oh? Why's that? It's not some palatial mansion, is it?"

"No, not that sort of thing...but, um, I'll do my best to make sure you can come over in two days."

"Not sure what you mean, honey, but I look forward to it."

Their casual conversation disappeared into Room 101. Soon, all the lights were off in the building, bringing a final, complete silence to the Sasazuka night right as the two AM hour passed.

THE HIGH
SCHOOLER
SEARCHES
FOR A GUIDE

As the lunch bell rang and the classroom brimmed with the excitement of sweet release, one student remained unmoving at her desk. Then, as the bell's final echoes faded, she slowly, gradually slumped over the desk, intractable as a stone.

"Hey, Yoshiya?"

"Huh?"

"Did you hear anything?"

Kaori Shoji, member of Class 2-A in Sasahata North High School, was chatting in hushed tones with her old friend and frequent collaborator Yoshiya Kohmura at his desk.

"What, about Sasaki?"

Yoshiya shook his head, keenly aware of what Kaori was talking about. In their eyes, Chiho Sasaki—fellow classmate, school club partner, and good friend since they all entered high school—had come to classes today with the will to live sucked out of her. She totally blanked out when her name was called during class. During breaks, she either slumped over her desk like now or wandered off to parts unknown.

It gave Kaori so much concern that she asked her what was up at the end of third period. "Sorry to make you worry," Chiho replied with an obviously contrived smile. "I just forgot my wallet, my phone, my memo pad, my pencils, and two of my notebooks at home, but it's okay." Anyone who knew Chiho knew that was *not* okay, as excuses went. The notebooks and pencils were one matter, but the rest of her lost items were the kinds of things that made you worry whether they were gone for good.

"If you don't know anything, it's not like I would."

"Yeah, I guess. But it doesn't look like she's eating lunch or anything..."

"If it's because she forgot her wallet, you or me could lend her some cash for today...but she usually brings her own bento lunch, doesn't she?"

"Not always..."

They got along well, but Yoshiya, involved with different clubs from Chiho and Kaori, wasn't together with them as often. Students usually wound up segregating themselves by gender during the lunch break. Chiho, Kaori, and a few other classmates would normally eat lunch together, and Chiho would bring her own food around 70 percent of the time.

"A bento lunch, huh...?"

"...What?"

"Oh, nothing related to you."

"Huh? The hell it ain't," the off-put Yoshiya replied after being dragged into this conversation. "I'm club president. If someone on the team's depressed about something, I think I gotta offer some help."

With all its senior members now gone, the Sasahata North High School *kyudo* club had a whopping three second-year participants—Chiho, Kaori, and Yoshiya. Yoshiya, defying the predictions made by every other member of the student body, was now club president. Most expected the role to fall upon either the stable, reliable, talented Chiho or the serene, caring Kaori, but Yoshiya nabbed it instead.

The reason was simple: Thanks to his netting a few fresh club members from the incoming middle school grads, Sasahata North's *kyudo* club barely managed to keep enough people to field a full five-person squad for team events. Thus, Yoshiya had four first-year boys and one girl to look after. "You got all those people under your wing," reasoned Kaori, "so why don't you just be club president? We can be your two vice presidents instead."

Chiho had no objections, so that was how things worked out back this summer. The summer school tournament later that season ended disappointingly, with Sasahata being eliminated at the semifinals in both the individual and team events—but they still made it that far in the team competition with Chiho shooting first and Kaori fifth and last, which was a decent achievement as far as club sports went.

As Kaori was recalling now, Chiho's lunch-eating habits had started to change around the summer period. She noticed because of how boundlessly fancy Chiho's bento meals became. She began bringing a large box to class around the tournament period, and its contents clearly had extra care applied to them, far more than just a bunch of frozen junk cobbled together.

"Hmm..."

"Shoji?"

"I think I might have an idea about this. I'll see if I can make her snap out of it before club activities start up again."

"Really? Best of luck!"

If Kaori claimed she'd do it, Yoshiya was willing to let her shoulder all the burden. Even the younger club members knew that leaving things to Chiho and Kaori usually worked out more smoothly. But it was also clear that Yoshiya's attitude—completely mindless to put it harshly, boundlessly optimistic to put it nicely—had a positive impact on the people around him. Compared to back in the spring, when figuring out life after graduation drove him half-insane, Yoshiya looked like a heavy weight was taken off his back. Chiho's sober dedication had a lot to do with that, but from Kaori's perspective, she wouldn't want Yoshiya any other way.

At the same time, dealing with Chiho when she's all clammed up like this couldn't be more difficult for her to deal with. She had to make her cough up whatever she was hiding in her shell, or it'd make everybody worry before long. So she sat down at the empty desk in front of the still-sprawled Chiho.

"Hey, Sasachi, you kinda under the weather today? Not feeling up for lunch?"

"...Nnnnno, no, I'm hungry."

The reply sounded more energetic (and self-serving) than she expected.

"Okay. There're probably no seats left in the cafeteria, so you wanna eat here? I heard you forgot your wallet, but you didn't forget your bento, did you?"

"No, I did..."

"Wow!" Kaori couldn't help but laugh. "Well, I'll have Yoshiya pay for it, so let's have some curry or udon noodles at the cafeteria. They oughta still have some left if we go now."

The battle to secure lunch at the Sasahata North High cafeteria was a constant struggle most days, but the school organized their purchases so there was always plenty of curry and udon on hand, often leaving quite a bit left after the initial rush subsided. They both cost a mere two hundred yen, making them easy enough to order even on a high school student's average allowance.

"..."

Chiho pondered a moment, head still against wood.

"I can't eat curry or udon. Anything but that today. I'd feel bad."

"Bad? What, for the curry and udon?"

"Yeah."

"Did curry or udon do something to piss you off?"

"...They've been a lot of trouble for me."

"Curry and udon have?"

"Yeah."

"So are you, like, actually the Soba Fairy and you refuse to accept blasphemy like curry and udon for lunch?"

"The udon party. Yeah."

"Ooh, pissed off by the udon party, huh?"

This not-quite-a-conversation continued for a while longer before Kaori finally heaved a light sigh, crossed her legs on top of the chair, and looked around. Yoshiya was already gone, perhaps out eating lunch with the other boys, and the bento-bringers left in the classroom were busy with their own chattering. Kaori surveyed her surroundings closely, then leaned in close, whispering to make sure only Chiho could hear her.

"You get dumped?"

"N-no!!"

"Ooph!!"

"Agh!! Nh!"

Chiho shot up, causing the back of her head to slam against Kaori's face. The subsequent rebound back to her desk landed a fairly severe blow to the tip of her nose. The force of the surprise impact made Kaori rear back, almost making her fall off her chair.

And so…

"Um, sorry."

"Me too."

The two were all smiles as they hung out in the nurse's office. The sight of two young women about to bud into adulthood, both bleeding profusely as they waited there, wasn't exactly charming. The nurse applied some quick first aid, and they were out once Chiho's nose stopped bleeding, walking down a corridor that the afternoon sun did little to light up.

"So…?"

"I have to tell you?"

"If you don't, let's go eat curry or udon."

"Oof…"

"What?" Kaori gave a confused smile. "Do you really hate them? That wasn't just an analogy or something?"

"It's kind of an analogy but not really. I don't hate them, but it's hard to face up to them, so…"

"Well, how 'bout we go outside?"

Kaori guided Chiho out to the school courtyard. A few boys from some other class were playing soccer in their school uniforms, sweating in their dress shirts despite the cold. A lot of them sported pants that were heavily worn around the cuffs; they must have spent a lot of afternoon breaks this way. The two of them leaned against the wall at one corner of the school, feeling around for something to talk about.

"If you followed me without complaining, you're willing to talk to me?"

"I guess you won't let me go until I do."

It was surprisingly difficult to find an area in school free of other people during lunch. You might think nobody would be up on the roof, but step up to the landing and you'd see groups of people relaxing or playing cards to avoid any snooping faculty. The competition for space was intense. The more specialized rooms, like the computer lab and home ec department, tended to get taken up by the clubs and other groups that used them a lot. In a season like this, it was much easier to find solitude outside.

"Whew… I dunno where to begin…"

"Well? Who is it? That guy from work?"

"Kao?! I haven't even said anything…!"

Having Kaori drive into the very heart of her issues before she could even formulate an introduction made Chiho physically leap into the air. It also made her realize there was no trying to dodge the question now. She fell to her knees on the landing, cowering down. Kaori had visited her at the Hatagaya MgRonald several times, even talking with "that guy from work" at least once, but Chiho hadn't told her much else about the workplace. She wasn't expecting such a pinpoint diagnosis.

"Ah, it's easy to work out my stuff with you, Sasachi. As far as what I could figure out, I was expecting to make you confess to it and beg for mercy as we were having curry or udon, but…"

"What kind of scenario is *that*?" Chiho attempted to complain, even as she realized that, given Kaori's experience, maybe her guess wasn't so out of the blue after all. "Lemme just say, though, I wasn't dumped or anything."

"Okay, so what is it, then?"

"…Um." Chiho chose her words carefully. "I wasn't dumped…but I kind of lost my temper."

"Lost your temper?"

"Yeah… Um, it was nothing…but between that nothing, a whole ton of stuff happened, and it felt like it threw everything up in the air for me."

"'A whole ton' sounds like a lot. And if you say there was nothing and it made you lose your temper, that sounds a lot like you've been dating that guy for a while, but now you're angry because he won't, like, go to the next step with you."

"N-no!" Chiho hurriedly replied. "It's not that! We aren't dating or anything!"

"You aren't? What was this guy's name again? He had kind of a weird one."

"Maou."

"Maou. Was that it?" Kaori shrugged. "It usually takes me a few repetitions before I remember someone's name. So why're you going on about nothing if you aren't even dating? Do those fancy bentos you had in the summertime have anything to do with it?"

"You noticed that?" Chiho asked, surprised.

"Well, yeah, they're totally a step above the rest of the class. Bigger, too."

"...Yeah, I gained some weight for a while thanks to that."

"Oh? Well, that's interesting."

Once the ice was broken and Chiho was ready to talk, she found Kaori's friendly tone irresistibly comforting.

The whole reason Chiho began bringing food to Room 201 of Villa Rosa Sasazuka was because Suzuno, who moved in that summer, started hanging out there all the time. Thanks to the mistaken notion that Suzuno might be falling for Maou as well, Chiho was suddenly burning to do something about it—but the new girl's cooking skills were admittedly far beyond the realm a high schooler like herself could reach. Taking the normal approach wouldn't be enough to overtake her, so for the first time in her life, Chiho undertook a crash course in finer cuisine.

Her mother, of course, saw through this almost immediately. She even told her father. He had mixed feelings about it, but her mother approved—"it saves me from thinking up a new menu every day," she said—and she wound up teaching her daughter quite a bit.

This marked the beginning of Chiho's demonic food donations, and truthfully speaking, her dishes took up maybe a third of all the food on the table at Devil's Castle. She underwent a long trial-and-error process at first, in search of a way to win out against Suzuno, and that often led to taking on more than she could handle in the kitchen and failing spectacularly.

She had first expressly confessed her love to Maou on that first day she brought meals over. It seemed like quite a while ago, but it hadn't even been half a year. The sweltering heat and the cicadas all seemed to melt away from that sweet moment in time, the way Chiho sensed it. It wasn't some spur-of-the-moment impulse or someone egging her on—it was her firm, indomitable belief.

As she thought, there was no better time to spring the news. Unlike earlier, when she was just beginning to foster feelings for him, she now knew quite a bit of his backstory. She knew it, and it didn't change her emotions at all. So she went out with it—out to the first man she ever loved in her life.

"Wow! Pretty scintillating!"

"...Don't pick on me. It's so embarrassing I could die."

Chiho had censored out everything involving Ente Isla, but the rest of her story was the truth. It made Kaori break out into an exaggerated whoop of delight. Despite the cold, her face felt warm to the tips of her ears.

"You know," Kaori said, "when I was in middle school, I just kind of assumed that everybody in high school is busy dealing with their boyfriends or girlfriends all day. But it really doesn't feel that way to me, you know? Or to a lot of people around us. It is with some people, but you know. So having a friend of mine lay it all bare to a guy like that... I don't think I've heard a story like that before."

"Ooh..."

"Aww, you're so cuuuuute, Sasachi! So what'd he say?"

After a love confession like that, anyone would be curious about the reply. But it only made Chiho's face darken.

"Well, that's one reason why I kinda lost my temper... I haven't gotten an answer yet, really."

"Whaa?!"

That reaction was no exaggeration.

"You told him during summer break, didn't you? Huh? It's December right now!"

"Yeah."

"So… You're still working at that MgRonald together and stuff?"

"…Yeah." Chiho nodded. They were together in quite a few other places as well, but she glossed over that. "I told him that I didn't want a response immediately, but…"

"Ohhh. Well, huh! Even so…you know? Ah, well. So that's one reason. Is there anything else?"

"Yeah, um…"

If Chiho wanted to go into any further depth, the topic of Alas Ramus would have to come up. She did her best to summarize the situation, taking care to avoid any Ente Isla–centric keywords. As she put it, Maou had kind of a drifter relative who left him with a child, an infant really, to take care of. As a high school student, Chiho couldn't offer much help to a single father trying to raise a kid.

"Well, yeah. If you do that and the teachers found out, you'd have to deal with a lot more than just the guidance counselor."

"Yeah. Our boss at MgRonald yelled at him over it, too, the whole 'Think about what society might think of you guys' and stuff."

Despite that, at Maou's fervent request, Chiho decided to do whatever she could reasonably offer to help out. However, the care of this child was eventually left to another woman.

"Ooh, here comes your rival, huh?!"

"Kao, stop acting like this is so much fun for you."

"What do you want? How could I be anything besides excited when this new cast member comes up?"

"Maybe, but…she's not really a rival exactly."

That would be Emi Yusa, an old acquaintance of Maou's and a single woman who wouldn't have any social stigma preventing her from helping out at his place. It was debatable how much enthusiasm she had for coming over, but in the end, the child wound up bringing Emi and Maou closer together (at least proximity-wise). It was Emi, as well, who had told Chiho all about Maou down to the slightest detail, in the end.

"She's a really strong, really pretty woman. Kind of a reliable big-sister type. We really like each other."

"...I can tell you feel that way, Sasachi, but this sounds like a huge drama pit."

They were old acquaintances, but Emi and Maou also had a great deal of trouble getting along. If it wasn't for the child, there were times when they wouldn't even want to talk to each other.

"So why is she so set on taking care of this child she isn't related to?"

"It's a long story, but let's just say she's got her motivations. For one, the girl really loves her."

"Ohh."

So the two didn't get along well with each other, but as their mutual friend, Chiho had always hoped they would find a way to make up sooner or later. Eventually, Emi lost her job following some personal issues, but thanks to her skills and proactive attitude, it wasn't long before she found her next one.

"Wait, don't tell me...?"

"Yeah. At the MgRonald me and Maou work at."

"Whoooaa. You're puttin' yourself through hell, girl!"

"It's not hell, really. I told him I loved him, but we're not exactly a couple yet. Me and Yusa get along pretty well, too, and really I'm glad she's on the team. We had kind of a staff shortage at the time, so I was the one who suggested to Maou that we should hire her on."

"Wow, again? Why?"

"Well, I figured maybe they'd mend things up a little if they worked together."

"Why are you creating this personal hellscape for yourself, Sasachi...?!"

"I told you, it's not hell! I'm not having a huge argument with Maou or Yusa or anything!"

"But what, then? If you're sure it's not a hellscape for you, then it's all working out just the way you hoped it would, isn't it? You're working with friends and people you like, and you aren't in a hurry for a response, although I really think you should press him a little, girl. You've factored everything in, yeah?"

"Yeah...pretty much, but..." Chiho looked down at the ground. "One of the veteran crewmembers is leaving the MgRonald. He's looking for a career job somewhere, but it made me think...like, everyone in our class better start thinking about entrance exams, too, huh?"

"Oh, yeah. A lot more classmates are going to after-school prep centers these days."

"But that guy leaving makes everything a little different from how it was before. You notice that his name isn't on the shift schedule anymore; you start getting assigned to different work stations in your own shifts… I started noticing those little changes, and I was like *oh, craaaaaap!* Like, it made me realize that I can't keep things like this forever."

"What do you mean, 'like this'?"

Chiho noted Kaori's quizzical look as she attempted to piece together all the thoughts she had gone over in her mind today.

"It's my next-to-last year in high school. I've grown up comfortably with parents who love me. I haven't had any big exam or other life-altering event. I go to school, hanging out with you and Kohmura and everyone, taking notes and eating lunch and practicing *kyudo.* When I go to my job, I can hang out with Maou and Yusa and Ms. Kisaki, and over at his apartment building, there's Suzuno, and Maou's friend Ashiya, and this guy Urushihara… And it all seemed like a given to me, but the other day, I realized, it's all a temporary thing. That finally struck home, I think."

"Right."

"So then I realized, I'll be like Kota someday, too. This day will come when I'll just disappear from someone's life. And when I think about that, these things I never cared at all about before get so important to me that I don't even know what to do."

"Kota's the guy leaving MgRonald?"

"Yeah. Um…Kotaro Nakayama is his full name. We use nicknames a lot around the kitchen, so I needed a moment to remember his real one."

"I hear you there."

"So then, after that, I started thinking about all kinds of stupid stuff at once…"

This nickname system was a deeply embedded part of the culture at the Hatagaya MgRonald. It wasn't anything forced; more of a case-by-case deal, with some going by their real names and others not. Chiho was Chi to everybody on the payroll except for Emi.

"But you know, among his circle of friends, I'm the only one Maou calls by a nickname. He calls Yusa 'Emi,' and his neighbor is just 'Suzuno,' but I'm still 'Chi' to him."

"Hmm."

A nickname isn't necessarily a sign of looking down on the person in question. Maou adopted the habit long before they had any deep relationship. But Kaori simply nodded at it without further comment.

"And I told you they don't get along, but really, he's way nicer to Yusa than he used to be. Like, he acts all curt and mean around her, but it's really just so Yusa can keep her pride intact more than anything."

"Mm-hmm, mm-hmm."

"But I'm the only member of this circle who's a student living at home, and I'll have college exams next year. I won't be able to see them nearly as often then...and..."

"And?"

"...And another acquaintance of Maou and Yusa's showed up recently...and she's offering a really huge job to both of them."

This "huge job" was, of course, the rescue of all Ente Isla's humanity at Laila's request, a detail Chiho thoughtfully omitted.

"Mmm, all right."

"We had all been together up to now, and I sort of assumed that could keep on going indefinitely. But it's not, and in fact, what I assumed was normal life for me actually isn't gonna last very long at all. And it kinda made me panic."

"Right, right."

Kaori nodded, crouching down next to Chiho and patting her on the back.

"Like, maybe Maou and everyone else are gonna be off somewhere before long. But I can't join them. I have to stay here, because he and I come from different worlds anyway. So I just... I wanted an answer, ASAP."

"Yeah."

"I wanted Maou and Yusa to get along all this time, but now it's, like, seeing Maou meddle with Yusa's affairs is so hard for me to watch. No matter what I do, by next year I can't be together with Maou and them all like I am now. And I know I'll only be busy with exams for a year. It'll be as short as this moment maybe. But if they decide to go and take on this big job…I don't really know how it'll turn out. I may not see them again for years. I'm so jealous of the people who get to stay with him. It drives me nuts."

"Yeah."

"But…I really love Yusa, too. But I'm getting all jealous over this stupid, pointless thing I can't do anything about, and it's, like, what am I even doing? This is exactly what I wanted for them, but no matter what I do…"

"Yeah!"

Kaori wrapped her arms around Chiho's shoulders. They didn't look at each other's faces. That was the rule.

"So I wonder, what even am I…to Maou?"

That was the small, ever so tiny, thornlike concern that had been jabbing away somewhere in her mind all this time.

"He's always looking out for my safety, I'm always dragging him down… I might be a major pain in the ass, for all I know, but maybe he's too kind to come out and say that. My thoughts go into this huge negative spiral, and I can't climb out of it."

She had confessed her feelings to Maou but not in the standard *Would you like to be a couple?* kind of way. All she did was say, in a person-to-person kind of way, that she loved him. That was why, even if she wanted a response, she wasn't even sure what kind she wanted.

"Not that I'd really know…but it sounds like you really enjoy these people, Sasachi. Maybe I'm a little jealous even."

"Oh, um, I'm sorry, I didn't mean it like…"

"No, I get it. They're them, and I'm me. I know a lot about you, Sasachi, that I bet they don't know about. So basically, you hate yourself for being jealous, but you still can't get your own emotions together, so you're freaking out. Is that right?"

"Yeah…"

"Your face looks awful. You got a handkerchief?"

"...No."

"Here's some tissues."

"Thanks..."

The tears had started rolling out again, along with some embarrassing nasal discharge.

"...And the worst thing is, I vented my anger at Suzuno."

"Ooh, that sounds bad. That was Maou's neighbor?"

"Right. I ran into her in town, and I was kind of falling apart back there, too, and before I knew it, we were at the Tacoma's Best in the station and she was trying to console me. Looking back, I really put her in this horrible place, but she heard me out all the way."

But as much as she understood Chiho's anguish, Suzuno had no answer for her. She went into several rants about how thoughtless Maou was, how much he was letting Chiho spoil him, but when it came to how their paths might diverge before long, she didn't have much to offer.

"Mmm. I see. Your lover isn't giving you an answer, you're getting all jealous of your best friend, and you complained all about it to this other friend of yours? No wonder you're kicking yourself over it."

"...Yeah. So that's why I'm like this today."

"All right. Well, I think I understand. Definitely goes beyond anything curry and udon could handle."

Kaori briskly nodded.

"So now what? Should I tell you what I'm thinking?"

"...If you have anything, I'm all ears."

Between Suzuno and now Kaori, Chiho hated how pathetic she must've looked, clinging to her friends like this. She had no idea where her own feelings lay any longer.

"All right. If you ask me, I think you should be a little more selfish."

"What do you mean?"

"Exactly that. Just grab Maou by the collar and demand an answer! Tell him you don't like how nice he's being to Yusa! What could go wrong?"

The suggestion was so provocative that it almost horrified Chiho.

"Wh-wha—? How am I supposed to do that?"

"Why not?"

"Why not? I..."

Yeah, why not? Why couldn't she do that? Was she forbidden to? Why?

"You never have before, huh?"

"I have, kind of, but..."

"I'm not saying you should deliberately start drama between you and Yusa, but if you're *that* buddy-buddy, I really think you're safe in telling her exactly how you feel. Say you want to date him, and like, you're gonna have *this* to deal with next year, but you wanna all be together for as long as you can. Because I don't really think there's any other way to solve this."

"Mmmmmmaybe."

"That's my main takeaway from all this. Also, I don't know how important Yusa really is to you, but if a guy you like is acting all nice toward someone else, of course that's gonna be frustrating to you. That's normal. And if you're getting all depressed because of this jealousy that Yusa herself isn't even aware of, that's just lame, girl."

"Oww..."

Provocative and merciless. Chiho had her suspicions about it, but having it stabbed into her like this completely sunk her battleship.

"It's lame because it makes you look like you're trying to be the only good guy in all this. People get jealous all the time, but a friend's always gonna be a friend. So what's the big deal? If it hurts your friendship, then...well, that was probably bound to happen anyway."

Suzuno hadn't offered her anything like this. It was merciless, but with Kaori saying it, Chiho had nothing to counter with. Coming from the same generation as her, it was the most bleedingly obvious thing.

"You've already confronted him once. Why's it gotta be so scary to do it one more time for keeps? And if Suzuno was *that* worked up about it, then you definitely gotta use her as your ally. I mean, procrastinating on a reply for four months is far too long."

"Y-yeah..."

"So I know that's all easy for me to say, not being involved. You're the one who makes the final call, Sasachi."

"...Right. Thank you. Sorry I'm being so incoherent."

"It'd be worse if you *were* coherent. I've got no love experience, so if you said something like your boyfriend's cheating on you, I would've fled hours ago. Oh, and I don't need regular updates, but once it's all settled, make sure to report back to me, okay?"

"All right..."

Sensing how serious-minded Kaori was about this, Chiho resolved to reveal one more shameful aspect of herself while she had her ear.

"Also..."

Kaori patted down her skirt as she stood, looking toward the school building. Following her gaze, Chiho saw the clock above the front door.

"Ah!!"

Now she understood Kaori's concern. The clock was cruelly, ruthlessly showing five minutes until the end of lunch break.

"We can talk about missing out on lunch later."

"Um, maybe when I have my wallet again..."

Chiho instantly felt hungry again, now that her feelings were all out in the open, but it was too late. She was forced to tackle the subsequent fifth and sixth periods on an empty stomach.

"Ahhh... I'm hungry..."

Upon returning home, Chiho collapsed into bed.

She did manage to borrow some money from Kaori so she could buy a roll from the nearby convenience store between sixth period and her *kyudo* practice, but for someone with an appetite like hers, a single roll would never fill her stomach. Having Kaori light a fire under her made practice just as chaotic for her, ruining her stance and breaking her arrows. Her stomach growled so loudly that the first-year students could hear it.

It was awful, given how she usually took a bold, measured stance at the archery range, but there was no way she could admit to skipping lunch after whining about her love life all day. Kaori, at least, played defense for her against Yoshiya and the rest. Between that and the roll she paid for, she'd be owing her for a while to come.

"Oh, right, my phone."

The phone, still plugged into its charger by the bed, reported a few missed calls and text messages.

"Huh? Mom?"

The calls were from her mother Riho, dated around the time school ended. She wasn't around when Chiho came home, likely for some errand or another. She gave her a call back, only to hear Riho half shout at her.

"Chiho, I called you a bunch of times this afternoon! Why didn't you answer?"

"Sorry, Mom, I left my phone at home this morning, so I didn't have it again until now."

"Ohhh. Are you at home?"

"Uh-huh."

"All right. There's an old classmate of mine that's in the hospital, so I'm meeting up with a few local friends and we're all going to visit him."

"Oh, okay. Is it bad?"

"It sounds like he broke some bones in an auto accident, sadly. Nothing life-threatening, but it'd be heartless of us all not to visit him. Today's about the only day that works for all of us, so we're all gathered in Shinjuku right now. It's not the hospital you were in."

"All right. I'll figure out something for dinner, then."

"Would you mind? I don't think your father will be home tonight, either."

"What about you? Are you eating with your friends?"

"That's the idea, although we won't be drinking. We all have work, so I shouldn't be too late. Thanks!"

"Okay, see you later! ...Hmm. Now what?"

After hanging up, Chiho buried her head in her pillow, dwelling on her thoughts. Breaking a sweat during *kyudo* practice made her extremely hungry, but she had expected dinner waiting at her house, so she turned down Kaori and Yoshiya's offer to stop by a café on the way home. Whether she ate at a restaurant or picked up something from the convenience store, she'd have to drum up the energy to go out again—but after today's events, she had no drive to whip something up from scratch. Something told her that her mind would start to race again while she started cooking.

"What to do…? Hmm?"

So while playing with her phone to delay the question, she came across a text from today's messages from an unexpected name, sandwiched between two coupons from Len and Mary's and MgRonald.

"That's rare. What's up?"

She skimmed the text, then immediately called the sender back. It was a dinner invite from Rika Suzuki.

It was just past six at Sasazuka station, rush hour only beginning as Chiho found Rika standing by the turnstiles, looking uncomfortably out of sorts.

"There she is. Hey, Suzukiii!"

"Oh, hi, Chiho! Sorry to call you out this late."

Running up to her, Chiho noticed that Rika was done up to the height of fashion, instead of sporting her usual casual wear.

"Was your family all right with this?"

"Sure. My parents are out all evening. Are you coming back from something?"

"Yeah, sort of," Rika replied, a bit vague. "So like I wrote you, would you be interested in dinner with me?"

"Sure, certainly."

Chiho couldn't guess why she texted her about it. She had grown fairly acquainted with Rika as of late, but if Rika was going to ask anyone out for a quick dinner, it'd be Emi first.

"Today," Rika added as if reading her mind, "I wanted to see you instead of Emi, so…"

"Really?"

She didn't mind the attention, of course, but it still seemed a bit off-kilter. Rika was dressed far more sharply than usual. She was always so bright and bubbly deep down, even when Gabriel and the Eastern Island forces attacked her (although she was no doubt scared, too), but today there was this bizarre pall in her expression.

"Let's figure out where we'll go first. I can't take you anyplace where alcohol is served, so it'll have to be a diner or something, but is that okay?"

"Of course. Anywhere's fine."

"Okay. Ready to go? I don't really know what's around here, but do you have any local recommendations?"

"Well..."

What kind of restaurants would a young office gal like Rika go to? It felt like a test of Chiho's tastes, in a way. She crossed her arms. It was hard to imagine Rika dolling herself up just to see her. Maybe there was something related to Emi or Maou she wanted to talk with her privately about. It'd have to be someplace that served food, was slow-paced enough that they could talk in peace, and allowed underage customers at night. That, and most importantly, the way today worked out had made Chiho almost unbearably hungry.

"I know!"

"Oh, you got an idea?"

"It's kind of a walk, but do you mind?"

"No, let's do it."

They walked a bit over ten minutes away from Sasazuka station, Rika idly asking about school and Chiho leisurely fielding her questions, until they reached Gyo-Gyo-En, a conveyor belt sushi joint famous for its standard hundred-yen-per-plate pricing.

"Oh, nice. That's a good choice."

Rika's expression told Chiho she had chosen wisely.

"Do you come here a lot? I know the name, but I've never been inside. It's kind of outside where I normally hang out."

"I've never eaten any *really* fancy sushi, but I definitely think you'll like it."

"Ooh."

"I haven't been here in a while, but I read an ad somewhere about their new high-end menu, so I figured now would be a good opportunity."

"Yeah, you see a lot of chains that began at one hundred yen per plate, then started charging two hundred for anything decent, or offering ramen and other nonsushi stuff or whatever."

"I don't know if they have ramen here or not," Chiho said, grinning as they opened the door. Fortunately, the evening rush hadn't hit here yet, allowing them to take over a booth by themselves.

"You should expect it to be pretty decent, though," she added as she wiped her hands with a towel. "Emeralda couldn't stop raving about it when she first came to Japan. I think she had a stack of almost thirty plates going."

"Whoa... That tiny woman?"

Rika's eyebrows arched upward in surprise for a moment before she grabbed a towel of her own and leaned back against her padded seat.

"Oooh, I'm exhausted. Sheesh."

"Did you go somewhere far away?"

"Nah. Really close in fact," she groaned as Chiho picked up her cup of green tea. "I was out on a date with Ashiya in Shinjuku."

"Wow, a date with...*ouch*!"

It took a few moments for her brain to comprehend Rika's statement. When it did, it made her spill a bit of piping hot tea on her lap.

"Ack! You all right? Did you burn yourself?"

"N-no, I'm fine. I'm fine, but *whaa*?! Suzuki, you were out on a date with Ashiyaaa...? *Really?!*"

"You don't have to act so surprised, Chiho. I'm a grown woman, you know. I go out on dates and stuff."

"Yeah, of course, that's not what I'm surprised about. I mean, a *date*? With *Ashiya*?!"

Combining *Ashiya* with *date* seemed about as absurd to her as combining *Urushihara* with *honest labor.* It shocked her so much, she lost her voice for a while.

"It's that unexpected?"

"...It really is, to be honest."

"*That* much?"

"Uhm, no, I'm not saying you aren't attractive or anything, Suzuki, but I've never heard of Ashiya going out anywhere besides the grocery store, the library, temp work, or to deal with Maou's problems."

"Oh, *that's* what it is?" Rika sat up, smiling. "This isn't the first time I've gone out with Ashiya. Maou and Suzuno were with us last time. I was joining them when Maou bought a new TV."

"But that's not what we're talking about, right? I mean, if you're on a d-d-*date* with Ashiya, then..."

"Right. Just the two of us."

"Wowww!"

With the mixture of surprises Rika had for her this evening, that was about the only appraisal she could offer.

"Well, I'm kinda glad you feel that way, actually."

"Oh? I'm sorry, I didn't mean to be so rude..."

"Nah, nah. You should probably apologize to Ashiya, not me. I don't know how he is at home, but outside he's so well put together."

"That I...know, yeah."

"But if that's how you responded, I guess word hasn't leaked out yet, huh?"

"About what?"

"You didn't hear anything from Maou or Suzuno?"

"From them? About this date?"

"No, not that. Like, I'm calling it a date, but it really wasn't that different from when we went TV shopping earlier. Ashiya finally purchased a mobile phone today. A *smartphone* even. I was his shopping advisor."

"Ashiya brought a phone?!"

It was as if the Earth was going to start spinning in the opposite direction. It amazed Chiho so much she almost dropped her cup of tea entirely.

"I guess he kind of felt the need for one already, because he asked me for advice during that TV run, too, but it all kind of got delayed. You know there was this and that, so..."

"'This and that'... That's certainly one way to describe it."

"Yeah, isn't it?"

In the time between Maou's TV purchase and today, Chiho had learned how to cast magic and faced mortal danger over it, while Rika had her entire concept of worlds and humanity ripped to shreds.

"He wanted to apologize to me about all the Ente Isla stuff and go into more detail about the stuff he didn't tell me back then. That kind of thing. So I said yes!"

"Ohh, all right."

"It was mostly the same as what you and Emi told me, but hearing it all from the demons' perspective was kind of fresh. Once he started rambling about which region had the strongest knights and how much pain Emi and Emeralda caused him, I thought my eyes were gonna glaze over, but..."

"I know what you mean. They told me a lot about the demon realm before they attacked Ente Isla, too. I don't want to show *too* much of an interest in it, out of respect for Yusa and Suzuno, but..."

"Oh, totally! Emi kept saying I didn't need to worry about it, but as a third party, it's kinda hard to know how to react to a lot of it."

Rika smiled warmly, let out a hefty sigh, and rotated her right shoulder around.

"Ugh, this is still aching a little..."

She sighed again as she tried to knead out the shoulder pain.

"What's up?"

"Ah, well, we had some stuff happen while we were out."

Now she was rolling her neck around, taking in deep breaths.

"Um, are you okay, Suzuki?"

"I'm pretty much back to normal now...but yeah. So anyway, we said our good-byes right before I met with you."

She had looked a little morose back at the station—but here, face-to-face in this brightly lit restaurant, Rika really didn't look that well. There was a lack of healthy pink to her skin, as if she was recovering from an illness. Chiho worried for her health.

"And, you know, I told him I wanted to be a couple, and I totally failed."

That would explain it. Chiho's thought processes, as well as the noise of the restaurant around her, all flickered out of existence. All that remained was Rika's flat expression as she so casually let it leak out.

"Wha...?"

Rika just smiled. "It was, you know, kind of a pain. But we

shouldn't talk about this on an empty stomach, you know? Let's order something."

Her eyes naturally turned toward the conveyor belt. Meanwhile, Chiho was still paralyzed. Her hunger now had no presence at all in her brain.

*

Maybe she put a little too much effort into it.

Rika gave a final check to her outfit as she waited for Ashiya at JR Shinjuku station's west exit.

"...This should work."

Even if it *was* only the two of them, it wasn't hard to figure out that their date wouldn't be the giddy, frivolous affair the term suggested. It involved an apology, some explanation, and some phone advice—none of which exactly suggested pulse-pounding romance.

She was in a beige trench coat and dress, holding a handbag she reserved for special outings and sporting a pendant on a thin gold chain she almost never wore. It was definitely a higher shade of fancy than what she picked for the office.

"Ashiya's probably gonna dress the same as always. I need to act like I'm taking the initiative here!"

This would be the first time she was alone with Ashiya since Gabriel took him away. Even in this season, where layering was a must, Rika wasn't enough of an innocent young maiden to expect Ashiya to spend any money on his wardrobe.

"I apologize for making you wait, Ms. Suzuki."

That was why, when she heard the familiar voice and still felt her heart race a little from it...

"Ah—ahh—ahhhh—huh?"

...she then felt it almost palpitate at incredible speed from the sight entering her eyes.

"I am sorry for keeping you in this cold. I am experimenting a bit with this outfit, so it took some extra time for me to prepare."

"Uh, no, um, I just got here; it's fine, but..."

"Is something the matter?"

"N-no, ah, uhm..."

Ashiya gave Rika an odd look as her pulse continued to quicken. She could feel all the simulations she had played out in her mind before coming here, partly in an effort to keep herself calm, instantly shatter to pieces. Nothing at all could have prepared her for this.

"I—I didn't expect you to wear a...a suit to this..."

He was wearing a sharply tailored, charcoal gray three-piece suit.

"Oh, this?" Ashiya smiled. "I had purchased it rather a long time ago, but this would be the second or third time I have worn it."

It was accompanied by a well-ironed dress shirt, a pair of brand-new leather shoes, and a perfectly positioned striped tie. The coat he had draped over one arm looked like a UniClo light fleece affair, but everything else he had on made him look like a model for a line of gentlemen's clothing, it was so perfectly suited for his tall frame and body shape. Rika, unable to slow her pulse, could feel the blood rush to her cheeks. This was *so* cheating. Talk about getting ambushed.

"I am so unused to this that I forgot how to tie a tie even. Very embarrassing. Hopefully there is nothing out of sorts with this?"

"No!" she reflexively screamed. "Not at all! You look soooo cool! I mean, I'm sorry my outfit isn't quite up to that level!"

A few moments ago, she was content in the fact that she didn't put too much effort into this. Now she was racked with regret. She should've put everything she had into her fashion from the start. Her coat was on the brink of everyday wear, something she took to the office now and then, and she couldn't even remember when she purchased the shoes she had on. She did like her handbag, but there was a small scratch on one of the pocket flaps.

But Ashiya just flashed a breezy smile and shook his head. "No, no, you have nothing to worry about. I am sure this has been nothing but a series of nightmares for you, Ms. Suzuki, and I had all but resigned myself to your refusing my offer. I truly appreciate you coming out here for me tonight. There is nothing for you to be sorry about at all. You are quite attractive."

"Eeee...!"

Rika's brain was already past the boiling point. She was usually never the sort of person to let pat compliments like *You are very attractive* get to her head, but there was nothing at all contrived about the way Ashiya put it. He really did find her attractive.

"Th-thank you..."

And if he did, the only way to answer that was with heartfelt honestly.

"So where shall we go, then? I do have a few things I would like to discuss with you forthwith, Ms. Suzuki, so I thought perhaps we could enjoy a meal somewhere first."

"Ah—ahh, um, sure! Please!"

The critical hit delivered by this ambush had wrecked all of Rika's plans. All she could do was nod at Ashiya's suggestion.

"Very good. I have a small list of candidates on hand..."

He took a neatly folded slip of paper out from an interior pocket. The mere act of seeing a man in a well-tailored suit take something out from his interior breast pocket was enough to make Rika's heart zoom into rapid-fire mode.

"There is an Italian restaurant down the train tunnel that has decent wood-fired pizza, and I read about an innovative Japanese place in the Lumina that offers an all-you-can-eat lunch special for *obanzai*, traditional cuisine from Kyoto. That, and a little walk away is a Russian restaurant known for its beef stroganoff..."

"Oh, that place closed."

Having something suddenly familiar thrust before her helped Rika regain enough composure to respond.

"Ah, did it? I suppose the site was out-of-date."

Ashiya must have looked up a restaurant review site and printed out a map with the results. He mentioned his inexperience with electronics before; he must've enlisted Urushihara or someone for help.

"I liked it a lot, too, but it actually closed just a little bit ago. It got replaced by a pasta joint, but I definitely wouldn't recommend them."

"I see. Come to think of it, you did live in the direction of Shinjuku, did you not? I'm sure you have a fine knowledge of the area, so if you have any suggestions my feeble attempts at searching failed to come up with, I would be glad to accept them."

"Oh, um..."

For a moment, Rika thought of the Manmaru Udon place she went to with Maou and Suzuno a while ago. She quickly shook it off.

"The *obanzai* place is perfect!"

"Is it?"

"Y-yeah," she replied, her hand toying with the handle on her bag. "Like, Italian is fine, but I don't want you spilling sauce on that fancy suit, Ashiya! I haven't been to that other place before, so...um... your choices are fine."

A familiar sort of frustration filled her heart. It was like she was back to being a teenage girl.

"Very well, then. Shall we?"

"Su-sure!!"

Ashiya gave her another sincere, nonaffected nod, then invited her to join him. To reach the Lumina from the west exit, it was fastest to walk down the subterranean mall next to the Keio Line turnstiles, then take the stairs to the left up a small ways. Being the lunch hour, it was a bit crowded around Shinjuku station as the two of them walked.

Rika noticed that Ashiya was casually taking care to match his walking pace with her own. Every time she spotted their reflection in a store window or mirror on the wall, she could feel something sweet throb inside her. They looked like coworkers in the same company or friends seeing each other for the first time in a while. That, or just two lovers out on a date. It made Rika recognize all over again that, even after learning the truth and having the most terrifying experience of her life, her feelings were still true.

Right now, she thought, *I know I love him from the bottom of my heart.* But even so, she couldn't quite will herself to hold the hand Ashiya dangled shortly ahead of her.

She continued to fidget just as nervously as they sat in front of the restaurant, shoulder to shoulder, and waited for a table to open. When it did, Ashiya removed his suit jacket, the sight of him in his prim vest quickening her pulse all over again. This constant rush of emotion was already starting to tire her out.

"Hmm…"

As Rika worried about whether she'd be able to keep her head on straight for their shopping trip, Ashiya intently peered at the menu.

"…Ah."

Rika took a peek at it as well. Then she spotted the prices. They made her raise her eyebrows a bit. Everything on the lunch menu was over a thousand yen, the priciest items pushing one thousand eight hundred. By Rika's standards, that was a lot to ask for lunch. She knew full well that Ashiya wasn't exactly rolling in it.

"Um, are you okay with this, Ashiya?"

If he had picked this place himself, he must have been aware of the cost. Still, considering his consternation when they were TV shopping, he might be stretching himself a tad too thin. It was a matter of pride, too, given that he had invited her to this. Rika thought a bit about how she could tell him—as lightly as possible, of course—that he didn't need to break the bank for her sake.

"Actually…"

Ashiya shook his head, eyes still on the menu.

"I was just thinking about whether I could prepare this golden eye snapper and boiled vegetables combo at this price."

"Huh? At home?"

"Yes. One thousand two hundred yen might seem high for a single dish, but it might be surprisingly hard to save any money cooking this myself, I thought."

"R-really?"

"Indeed." He placed the menu down and nodded, face cold and calculating. "The snapper itself is not an inexpensive fish. Seafood has been on the rise across the board lately. I would conjecture that a single fillet alone would cost three hundred yen."

"Ahh."

"In a restaurant like this, it is safe to assume that each customer will order something different. In the family kitchen, however, that isn't possible—not with the time and equipment your average family has to work with. I have three people to cook for, counting myself, so that would be three fillets at nine hundred yen. Plus, this is all-you-can-eat *obanzai*, complete with a small bowl of rice and miso soup. Free refills on the rice as well, I may add. If I attempted the same offer in Devil's Castle, the three of us would exhaust our rice supply in short order. I imagine this restaurant sells a given number of these snapper combos per day, but serving the same dish daily at home will simply not cut the mustard, so to speak. As a result, the amount of work and money it would take to duplicate this dish for a single meal would likely go far beyond expectation. That is why I thought, perhaps, one thousand two hundred yen is actually quite an appropriate price point."

"Wow, yeah. Never really thought of it that way, but..."

Rika was dumbfounded at first, but the nerves faded as Ashiya began to act more and more like his normal self.

"Oh, and I know it is normally my creed to scrimp and save as much as possible, but since you've made the effort to join me, Ms. Suzuki, there is no need to be concerned about such matters today. Times like these are exactly why I engage so enthusiastically in thrift."

"Sure. All right. Just make sure you don't make Maou mad, okay?"

Rika, it turned out, had nothing to worry about from the start.

"I will keep that in mind. Well... Now, then. Where should our conversation begin, I wonder?"

"Aw, no need to be too formal. I've already heard a lot about what happened after Urushihara showed up and what went on in Ente Isla and stuff. I'd like to know what went on after you got kidnapped, though."

"After that? I did hear word from Ms. Sasaki that you were in ill health for a while. Did you recover well?"

"Ah, you know how much of an optimist I am at the root of it! Chiho and Ms. Ohguro really looked out for me back there. Plus, I know the whole story, and I'm still going out with you today, right, Ashiya? You get the picture."

"Mm. Very well. I interrogated Gabriel and the Inlain Jade Scarves in detail afterward, but none of them had any word about what happened to you. I was quite worried. And in fact..."

And so Ashiya began to recall what happened after Gabriel kidnapped him, an event that had everything to do with Emi's own trip to Ente Isla. Rika listened, a calm, collected smile on her face. Much of it was a bit too difficult to grasp in the first repetition, but essentially everyone Rika cared about was safe and sound, and with Emi's mother back and possessing just the info they needed to tackle the riddles Ashiya couldn't quite grasp earlier, they had a great deal to look forward to.

"Sounds like quite an ordeal, but in the end, everyone's one step closer to their goals, huh?"

"Indeed. Although, perhaps not in a way I anticipated back when the Devil King's Army was alive and well."

"Yeah, and I doubt myself a year ago would ever seriously believe any of this nonsense, either."

Their orders arrived soon after, driving their conversation in the direction of food, Ashiya's and Rika's daily routines, matters around the workplace after Emi was fired, and other little trivialities.

Between Maki Shimizu and the rest of her coworkers, Rika had no lack of fun friends to eat out with, but *this* lunch outing felt totally different. Ashiya was talented at driving a conversation forward, and he was a good listener to boot. It was kind of funny how talkative he got whenever the topic veered toward Maou, Urushihara, their battle against Emi, or the Devil King's Army of the past.

"Regardless, considering our ongoing issues with Urushihara, we need to keep the running phone costs at an absolute minimum."

It was a given for Ashiya that he had to factor Urushihara's embezzlement habits into whatever he bought today.

The secret behind the very non-demon-like suit came out as well, in the midst of their talking. A little bit before Maou was hired at MgRonald, the two of them each purchased a suit at a menswear store offering a "buy one, get the second for one thousand yen" deal, figuring they might take on jobs in the future that required more formal wear. They never did find that job, so the outfits had spent most of the past year mothballed in the closet, accompanied by a pair of black and white ties for formal occasions.

"With the store's stock, they had a rather limited selection for someone of my height, so my liege was forced to purchase the thousand-yen suit instead. It is something I regret to this day."

"Well, not much you can do about that. Without a deal like that, the second suit probably would've cost twenty or thirty thousand yen otherwise, wouldn't it?"

"Indeed. And come to think of it, this may be the first large purchase I've made for myself since."

"Oh? Well, you oughta get something decent for yourself, then. Do you have any models or brands you're aiming for?"

"Not at the moment, sadly..."

"Ah. Actually, all the companies changed their pricing plans a little after you bought that TV. I think the types of phones you'd be best able to deal with are..."

After dinner, now fully used to the presence of Ashiya, Rika took a pen and memo pad out of her bag and shifted completely into work mode. After quizzing Ashiya on what he was looking for, this was her conclusion—

"So you want to go as cheap as possible. You can use that Idea Link thing as long as the handset works as a phone at all, so you aren't picky about brand or model. You're mainly using it for voice calls but not very long ones. The only people you're likely to text with it are the people who live in your apartment building. No plans to move outside large urban areas. You don't download games or music, but you might want to access the Net fairly often. Does that all sound right?"

"Yes."

"Okay. Sounds good. It's kind of a pity Emi didn't say something when Maou had to switch phones earlier...but I don't know much about AE, and I guess Maou's been with that carrier for a while. Maybe he had his own reasons for going with another feature phone like that."

Rika looked over her notes one more time.

"So if we're going to buy a phone without any monthly payments, how much are you willing to spend?"

"Monthly payments?" a confused-looking Ashiya asked. "Indeed. If I paid out everything I had, I think I could manage fifty thousand yen...although I understand most people pay by the month for things like this."

"Yeah, some of the newer phones go for a ton of money these days.

A lot of customers go for monthly payments on their phones on top of their regular bill, but if you go that way, you're gonna have to shell out at least six thousand yen a month."

"Six thousand a month..." Ashiya visibly soured. "My liege's monthly phone bill teeters around the four-thousand mark, so I was anticipating approximately that..."

"Mmm, I dunno when she bought it, but if Emi paid for Maou's phone in one lump sum, it's that much less he pays monthly, of course. Feature phones don't use up a ton of data for anything, so that's probably about right. But, for example, if you buy a fifty-thousand-yen phone and go for a two-year payment plan, that's gonna be a little over two thousand a month, just ballparking it. You're a new customer, Ashiya, so you won't get a loyalty discount, and Maou doesn't count as family, so you can't share a common plan. Factoring all that in, even six thousand a month might be kinda optimistic. It might go up a little, depending on which one you choose and how you wind up using it."

"Hmmmm..."

"So that's why I thought I'd ask whether you want to buy the phone in one payment."

"Oh?"

"Roughly speaking, if you buy your phone outright, there's a way to keep the monthly bill at three thousand or below. It's not very common, but..."

"Not very common? Do I need to perform some kind of complex operation with my device?"

"Nope. I only mean it's not very common to see in Japan yet. It requires a smartphone, too, so if you aren't up for that, it ain't gonna happen. You gotta buy the phone outright, and your carrier won't assign you a static e-mail address, so the longer you've been using your account, the harder it is to switch over to this. Along those lines, Ashiya, as long as you can afford the device, you can go with that right off."

"I'm not sure I follow everything you just said, but is this something you might be able to assist with as an employee, Ms. Suzuki?"

"Nothing like that. I'm not a full-time employee, and *this* is something open to anybody if they want it. And even though it's cheaper, it doesn't degrade the features and services available to you."

"Then why isn't it more commonly used?" Ashiya asked.

"Oh, a lot of reasons. It isn't advertised a lot. Japan's phone markets evolved in kind of a unique way from elsewhere, and this wasn't even available in Japan until recently, so it's only gotten started. But it's nothing you have to worry about, Ashiya. All that matters is whether you want to purchase a phone outright or not. If you don't think that'll happen, you might be able to find a cheaper plan that restricts what you can do, but..."

"No. The creed of Devil's Castle is to keep ongoing costs at a minimum. If my monthly fee can become that low and you say it is accessible to me, I have no reason not to pursue it, Ms. Suzuki."

"Great. Unless you want something else here, let's go find someplace selling Dokodemo phones."

"It will be a Dokodemo contract?"

Rika thought a bit over how to explain this to the technologically backward Ashiya.

"Not exactly, but you could kind of say it is, if you're willing to fudge the details. Have you ever heard of an unlocked phone before?"

"Unlocked how?"

"Um, how 'bout I fill you in on the way there?"

Rika stood up and grabbed the bill from the table out of habit.

"Oh, allow me."

Ashiya's hand landed on top of hers as he attempted to snatch it away.

"Huh?! Ah! B-but?!"

"I invited you here today to apologize, and I wanted to enlist your help after this. Please allow me."

"...Okay..."

The sense of calm that prevailed after all that phone talk vanished once more as Rika pulled her hand back. Ashiya gave this a satisfied nod, putting his suit jacket back on as he headed for the register.

Looking on from behind, Rika tightly clutched her right hand in front of her chest, as if trying to embrace the feeling of this man's large, slightly rough hand against hers.

"My, it has certainly grown dark, hasn't it?"

"Yeah. It's only five, too."

It was almost five o'clock sharp by the time they left the phone shop. Ashiya, quick to take action once his mind was made up, had fully purchased a slightly outdated Dokodemo smartphone, unlocked at Rika's recommendation. The store then set him up with a monthly service contract, providing the Dokodemo SIM card that hooked the device up to the Net.

Reaching this point, however, was an odyssey. The only electronics Ashiya interacted with were home appliances, calculators, and TVs, and now he was trying to purchase a smartphone. When the salesman explained that he could download a pdf manual if he couldn't figure out to use it, the color drained from his face. Realizing that he wouldn't even use the phone if left at sea like this, Rika dragged him up to the shop's upstairs café and gave him an impromptu lecture, beginning with how to turn the phone on.

As part of this, Rika opened up her phone book app, complete with her name and number right at the top. Maybe that didn't mean anything to Ashiya, but to Rika, it was an unexpected miscalculation that filled her with joy. Even that fright she received when Ashiya took the bill began to ease itself, with her growing gradually more used to brushing against his hand as they handed her phone back and forth.

With a couple of well-timed breaks in between, Ashiya had learned how to make calls, send and receive texts, add and dial numbers, and use the map and train schedule apps—all within a mere two hours.

"Boy, you might already be better than Maou at this, huh?"

"His Demonic Highness is one thing, but now that we are in the same arena of smartphones, I could hardly allow myself to lose out to Emilia."

Rika couldn't guess what kind of battle he meant to wage in this "arena," but it was cute to see him act all cocky again. By the time he mastered the map app, he was clearly getting used to the whole thing, his enthusiasm resembling that of a small child in a tall man's body.

But this fun moment came to an end all too quickly.

"Well, I do apologize for making you do all this for me. Thank you so much for everything today."

It was five PM, the sky already a deep shade of blue. The househusband had to go home and perform his family duties.

"...No, um, I'm just glad I could help you out."

She knew from before that he had evening responsibilities at home. She had assumed they had a lot more time than this.

"Indeed you did, Ms. Suzuki. Without your aid, I doubt I could have ever purchased and set this up by myself."

"Yeah." She nodded back.

"You live in Takadanobaba, correct? Perhaps I could take you there..."

"N-no, I'm fine. It's not dangerous or anything, and I know you have to get home soon."

Ashiya began to walk off, his hand barely too far away from hers, but the station turnstile just too close for her tastes. It felt like they had been to a thousand places, but Shinjuku station wasn't even a ten-minute walk away. Seeing the turnstile where they met made Rika feel like a kindergartner back from an afternoon field trip. The fun was over, her friends leaving the bus one by one, and she was all alone and feeling vaguely rueful about it all.

Something in her said she didn't want this to end. The feeling would be weirdly gone once she was back home, but the way back felt so painful. It wasn't like she'd never see Ashiya again—with everything she knew, it seemed fair to say they were closer together than before. But they lived in different parts of Tokyo. They quite literally came from different worlds.

Then she recalled someone else. Someone they all knew. Someone who deliberately, by her own will, chose to stand strong with all these people.

"Um, hey!!"

Ashiya looked beady eyed at Rika as she stood in front of the station entrance, yelling at him.

"Hey, um… Do you have maybe just a little more time?"

"Er, yes? Yes. A little."

"Okay, um… Umm, I just…want you to listen for a bit."

"Listen to you? Should we perhaps go somewhere more private for this?"

"No, here's fine."

The western exit was starting to fill with rush-hour commuters and people setting off to explore the city.

"Do you mind if I ask something…a little weird?"

"What is it? If it is that strange, I think I have already asked a great number of strange and bizarre questions today."

"Well, I expected that. This is the first time for you, so it's fine to act like a beginner. But it's not about that."

She had reflectively smiled, but looking up at Ashiya's face, she realized—her own was so tensed that Ashiya felt it best to try loosening her up a bit.

"Not about that, but… You know, about Emi…"

"Emilia?"

"Yeah. Half human, half angel, right?"

"It seems so, yes."

"Which means that on Ente Isla humans and angels can get married…can't they?"

"I suppose it is so. Certainly no need to wrangle with the local government office and go through all the name change bureaucracy, I imagine."

"All right…so…"

Her heart was pounding scarily fast, harder than ever before this day. In one corner of it, she apologized to her friend for planting the idea in her head.

"So," her trembling voice began, "can demons and humans… come together that way?"

"………Er?"

Even Ashiya found himself lost at this transition. He frowned a little as he thought over how to scrutinize this. A few moments of confusion later, he opened his mouth.

"...To be frank with you," he carefully intoned, "I am not sure I follow. Unlike humans and angels, demons come in a great variety of species and individual forms, each with differing body types, physiques, even shapes and organ structures. Perhaps it would be possible with the more humanlike races, but I am not aware of any concrete example, so I am unsure what to say..."

He scratched his head, worried about where to go from here.

"Honestly, I am somewhat surprised to hear the question from you, Ms. Suzuki. Since I have actually had my own thoughts about humans and demons, as of late."

"Huh?"

"Regarding Ms. Sasaki, I mean."

"Chiho...?"

The sound of Chiho's name from Ashiya's pained-looking face filled Rika with a foreboding unrest.

"Ms. Sasaki continues to have deep feelings for my liege, even after knowing everything there is to know about our past. Not long ago, however, there were concerns voiced over whether my liege is allowing himself to be too spoiled by Ms. Sasaki's goodwill. It led to some conflict within our apartment building."

"Maou's being spoiled by her?"

"She is a very wise young woman, so she never becomes emotional or blindly devoted to him as she deals with my liege. She deals with us fully aware of the anger and hatred all of Ente Isla's humanity foster against us, so she often sides with Emilia and her friends on matters. But...if relations between my liege and Emilia were to falter again, I am sure Ms. Sasaki would side with His Demonic Highness, in the end."

"Oh?" Rika interjected. "That wouldn't necessarily be the case..."

"I am sure that is what my liege thinks to himself, too."

"...Huh?"

"What I mean is, my liege has offered a great support to all of us. To Bell when she was just getting used to life in Japan, to you when you became caught up in our crisis, and to Emilia when she was targeted by intrigues in Ente Isla. But his care for Ms. Sasaki has been, shall we say, comparatively lacking. He claims to care about her as her boss and coworker, but one step away from MgRonald, and it is Ms. Sasaki's generosity that has helped him countless times, not the other way around. I fear his recognition and understanding of that was rather too shallow."

If Ashiya was willing to go that far, he must have been absolutely sure of it.

"To put it in a kind way, he trusted her broadly in all areas. In a bad way, he was spoiled. Either way, Ms. Sasaki is the only person His Demonic Highness will fully open his heart to. That was true, perhaps since even before Urushihara came here to confront us."

"And…so that's why, after the battle with Urushihara, Chiho was the only one…"

"Indeed. The only one whose memories my liege did not erase. And I did find it rather strange back then. It is easy to imagine now that she meant something special to my liege even at the time. A special relationship, one that continues to this day. And so, I have come to think as of late, I would appreciate it if you did not speak of this to others, however…"

He brought a hand to his chin.

"If my liege decided to make Ms. Sasaki his partner…or, in other words, his wife, what would happen then?"

"His—his—his *wife*?!"

The raw energy of that keyword struck Rika dumb.

"Such was my concern about this issue, you understand. But… well, I would hardly declare myself capable of reading His Demonic Highness's mind. If it comes to that, we can consider the issue then, I trust… Er, what were we talking about?"

"…Ah, um, uhhm, whether demons and humans can get married?"

"Ah, yes, yes. So what about it?"

"Well…"

Well, indeed. After a conversation that stark and unfettered, it almost felt easy now. Easy to say, that is. The words came out like a river.

"Well, kind of like Chiho and Maou, I...I think I've started to really like you, too."

"Ah..................huh?"

Ashiya nodded his understanding as always...then froze.

"Meaning..."

"I like you. A-as a woman."

"But...Ms. Suzuki, I..."

"I know. I totally understand how Chiho feels. I'm not asking to be your girlfriend or your wife or whatever; it's not like that. But I just thought I wanted to tell you. That I *had* to. I wanted you to look at me that way."

All her senses were finely honed now, all sounds silenced except the ones she and Ashiya made.

"Is that bad?"

"......"

Ashiya looked at Rika, face as stern as hers. But when their eyes were about to drift apart, Ashiya took his freshly purchased phone out of his pocket.

"Give me one moment, please."

"Okay."

He opened up his phone book with halting swipes and taps, then brought the phone to his ear.

"........About time. If you are glued to your computer anyway, I want you to answer the phone immediately... Yes. Alciel... I did. Add this number to your list. I will be slightly late returning home. My liege is working late tonight, so if you need to, eat whatever you want... Hmm? Pfft. So be it. Do what you like. But if you leave any food out on the table, you will pay dearly for it. Farewell."

Rika could tell who that terse conversation was with. Urushihara, no doubt, holding down the fort over at Villa Rosa Sasazuka.

"...My, I must be losing my composure. Urushihara threatened to have pizza delivered, and I actually said yes to him."

"...Sorry about that."

Rika didn't have much to defend herself with. Ashiya sighed, thrust the phone back in his pocket, and looked at her.

"Would you…mind coming with me for a bit?"

Ashiya strode slightly ahead of Rika as they walked down the tunnel. Judging by their direction, they seemed to be heading for the Tokyo Metropolitan Government Building, forcing them to wade through the crowds of workers going against them. Soon, they were back on the surface, amid the high-rises that marked Tokyo's business center.

He stood there for a moment, scoping out his environment. "This way," he finally said, inviting Rika away from the road. The wind around Nishi-Shinjuku, lined with corporate headquarters and five-star hotels, was powerful—and even colder, Rika felt, than when they left the phone shop.

"Where are we?"

They had stopped in the open patio area of a now-closed café sandwiched between two large buildings. Its opening hours were probably matched with the offices it shared this block with. Nobody was around.

Ashiya turned toward the incredulous Rika.

"Excuse me a moment, Ms. Suzuki."

"Huh? Ah! Whoa!"

Then he grabbed her by the hand and brought her closer to him.

That alone would have been enough to make Rika's heart explode, but he wasn't done. Her feet were leaving the ground. Before she knew it, she was being carried in his arms.

"Wha—wha—wha—wha, Ashiya? I— Wha-what're you…?!"

"Hang on tight, please. Keep your mouth closed so you don't bite your tongue."

"My, my tongue? Why're you…?"

She had no way to execute the whispered instructions before it began.

"Whoaaaaaaa?!"

The next moment, Rika was experiencing the Shinjuku cityscape like never before—from the sky.

"Hyeeeeeeegh?!"

She hugged her arms around Ashiya's neck—a fairly standard response for someone at as high an altitude as her.

"Wha—wha—whaaaaaa—?!"

"Right. That is the most stable way. I will be moving a little, so hold on."

"Ah—ah—ah—ah—ah..."

She was flying the friendly Shinjuku skies, safe in Ashiya's arms. In a film or something, this probably would've been a magical, fantastical, romantic situation, but getting thrown into this scene without warning as a human being incapable of flight, Rika couldn't do much apart from tense up her facial muscles and hang on for dear life.

It *was* beautiful down there. And she couldn't complain about her beloved holding her tight like a fairy-tale princess. But between the height, the cold, and the suddenness, it was maybe a little too much stimulation all at once.

Thus, unable to enjoy this scenario that every little girl in the world has dreamed of at least once, Rika found herself plunked down on the roof of one of the taller buildings in the neighborhood.

"Haah...haah... You totally freaked me out there...!"

"I apologize. I felt the need to be as far away from other people as I could manage."

"Where...is this?"

"The roof of Tokyo City Hall."

"Of *what*?!"

Rika shot to her feet in a cold sweat, looking around.

"Wh-why?!"

"I needed a large, open space with nobody else in it," Ashiya replied with a smile as he began to walk a distance away from Rika across the large windblown heliport.

"Ashiya?"

"I am very happy to hear about your feelings for me."

"Um?"

"It is a surprise for me, as well. I used to think of humanity as lowborn vermin worthy of nothing but contempt, but when I learned of your feelings, Ms. Suzuki, it did not discomfort me one bit."

Shinjuku at night was bright enough to blot out the moon itself. Ashiya began to blend in with the shadows.

"Sadly, though, I have no way of reciprocating those feelings. That is because..."

The wind was laden with a dark, heavy chill, just as it was when Ashiya invited Rika into the alley before. It now seemed to Rika that Ashiya was fully lost in the shadows, as absurd as she knew that was. This was a wide-open, flat roof. It had to be bathed in moonlight right now. But before she could figure out why it was so, a dark shade enveloped Ashiya as a howling gale coursed across the roof.

"Ah, agh!"

Rika fell to the ground as she felt a sudden tightness in her chest. This was no sweet, refreshing feeling driving her heart any longer. It was a pain like nothing she felt before—like she was given poison to drink, robbing her of the air she needed.

"Wh...what...?"

"...Because there is no such thing in this world as a man named Shirou Ashiya."

"—?!"

From the shadow Ashiya disappeared into, there arose a voice like none she had ever heard. It was low but still mighty and grating upon her ears.

"Are you in pain? This form, this power is what I truly wield, human. Everything you have seen before is a false body, a false name, to allow me to blend in with humanity."

She forced her face upward, gasping for breath, only to find a figure there larger than the one before. The glinting from its eyes as it walked forward made Rika shake, despite her will. It was a reaction driven by fear, the primal emotion that no human could ever fully shake off.

"My name is Alciel. A Great Demon General, a demon that no human can ever even set foot near. If you wish not to die, keep your distance. Our demonic force can easily take the lives of a human, weak as you all are."

Standing before Rika was a creature like none she knew, covered in a black shell. This armored carapace completely enveloped its

body, its twin-pronged tail waving ominously in the air, the dully glowing eyes staring right at her.

"Ah…Ashi…ya…"

"The humans who dwelled on Ente Isla kneeled before me in terror at my form. And we will return one day to make them acquiesce to our will."

"Ng…gh, haah!"

Nausea and tears welled up within Rika as she finally collapsed in a heap.

"Do you understand? Understand how foolish, how misguided, how much of a folly your feelings are?"

"Nn…nnggh…"

Her joints began to ache, as if she suffered from a high fever. It was growing difficult to even look straight at him.

So this is a demon? This demon she had heard about multiple times but never actually saw for herself? These people who killed and ruled over humanity on some faraway world?

Fending off the fearsome pressure and terror assaulting her body, Rika's mind began to whir into motion.

"Wh…why…?"

"Enough of your inane queries. I suggest that a human woman like you never make the same foolish mistake against a higher-level demon like—"

"Why did you show that to me…?!"

"………What?"

"I can't breathe… I—I heard about it, but I didn't think it'd be so—so rough… Gehh… I couldn't come near you if I tried. I can't move my legs…"

But even so, Rika drummed up enough willpower to look up and speak before the horrifying demon could answer.

"Thank you…for showing me who you really are."

"…!"

For one second, the confusion in Alciel's mind made its way to his face.

"If I was misguided… If I was in the way… You could erase my memories, couldn't you? I heard about that. So why…?"

"..."

"I'm scared. This really hurts. I don't want to go anywhere near you. I don't know what to do...but..."

Rika was unable to wipe the flowing tears away.

"But I still love you. No matter how much you try to scare me. No matter what awful things you say to make me go away. I know how kind you really are. That's why I love you. It's not me being misguided."

"..."

"You took me here...to keep from hurting other people, didn't you? You stepped away to keep me from—from danger."

Her pleading was mostly screamed out at this point, but it was odd how that first instant of pain seemed to relax itself now.

"You showed this to me because you wanted to give a serious reply to my feelings, didn't you?"

Alciel simply looked at the shouting human, face not moving a muscle. He could come no closer to the desperate woman. Only in his eyes could there be found an inexplicable sort of agitation.

"I knew that. I knew that...I could never be your lover or anything... but I can still say it now. I love you. I love you for using your precious store of power to give me a sincere no. That, I'm positive, was no mistake of mine."

But she had reached her limit.

"Thank you...Alciel..."

And just as there was that final, fleeting image of her lover from another world—in his true form, to her—she fell into darkness.

❈

"Yeah, so that happened. The next thing I knew, I was on a bench in Shinjuku Central Park. Ashiya was back in human form, and he kept on apologizing to me, so it actually got a lot more awkward. Like, I think it woulda been a lot better if he simply disappeared into the night, all mysterious-like, you know? But he said if something happened to me, Emi would've killed him and he woulda had no defense for it. So there he was, regular old Ashiya, none of the dignified demon stuff from before, and seriously, it made me feel so embarrassed for what I said to him. Hey, um, aren't you hungry, Chiho?"

"Ahh..."

Chiho's empty stomach was no longer a concern to her. Rika's story was enough to overwhelm her completely. Rika, meanwhile, was stacking up the sushi plates as if she hadn't just experienced a cross-world dumping.

"I know it sounds really silly, but you know how big demons get when they transform, yeah? He actually went behind that shadow to strip down beforehand so he wouldn't wreck his suit, he told me. I asked about his underwear—which I *know* is the stupidest thing to ask ever—and he said they were elastic enough that they were okay, which totally made me laugh. Like, that's *so* Ashiya for you."

"Ahh..."

"And then we said good-bye just now, at Shinjuku station. I could've gone home, but I didn't want to be in my room alone right after dealing with this insane broken heart, so as much as I hated to do it, I figured I'd give you a call, Chiho."

"Ahh..."

All Chiho could do was nod, holding a cup of tea that had long grown cold in both hands.

"And, you know, I heard that demonic energy was bad for you, but actually feeling it for myself, holy *crap*, it was rough! My joints hurt, I had this chill up my spine, I was nauseous... It totally wrecked me. It took this whole dinner for me to recover, really."

"Recover" was the way she put it, but judging by the color of Rika's face, the recovery process had only begun. In Chiho's case, it took a good night's sleep for all the aftereffects to go away. Whether that was because the Devil King was that strong or the combined forces of Maou, Ashiya, and Urushihara were too much at close range, she didn't know—but she remembered full well how, if it weren't for Emi's protection, she could have very well suffocated under the strain. Receiving treatment from Suzuno afterward—and learning holy magic for herself—made Chiho inextricably involved. But even so, that first instant of being exposed to the Malebranche's evil force still felt supremely uncomfortable to her nerves.

Rika, meanwhile, had no protection and faced the brunt of that force until she lost consciousness. And strangest of all, as far as Chiho was concerned, was Ashiya transforming before her eyes, despite claiming he had no need for demonic force in his regular life, after returning from Ente Isla. By her understanding, demons like Maou needed to retain at least a given amount of force within their bodies to perform the transformation. Maou used what little force he had remaining upon falling into Japan to establish a life for himself, but the effects of that cost him his original form, turning him into the regular human being Chiho knew well.

It meant, in other words, that Ashiya had been keeping enough demonic force to transform this whole time, in secret. Perhaps it was out of an abundance of caution—maybe he didn't quite believe everything about Gabriel or the heavens closing up—but then he would've told someone. It didn't seem to Chiho that Maou or Urushihara had any idea—or were they just not telling Chiho about it?

"..."

She immediately dismissed the idea. After all, if all three of those demons were keeping it a secret, that wouldn't explain why Ashiya revealed his true form to Rika. Did Ashiya always plan to scare Rika out of her feelings for him? If so, it meant he knew about Rika's love and prepared the required demonic force for the act in advance. But that didn't sound like the Ashiya that Chiho knew, and it'd contradict Rika's story.

To Ashiya, the love confession came completely out of left field. He was a kind person, and in order to nip her feelings in the bud, he tapped the demonic force he happened to have around for some reason and made the terrifying transformation he did. If Rika was to be believed, this explanation sounded much more like Ashiya's approach.

But if so, what was that "some reason"? It made even less sense. Ashiya knew that Rika was on good terms with Emi, Chiho, and Suzuno. If Rika told them that Ashiya had enough demonic force left to transform, that'd set Emi and Suzuno on guard again, right when they were starting to soften their stance a little. There was no merit to the demons antagonizing their old enemies all over again.

Chiho didn't get it. And as the inscrutable anxiety crashed over her again, Rika let out a heavy sigh.

"Man, I'm stuffed. This place is really good! I guess a hundred yen still gets you a lot more than I thought."

"Oh, um, great..."

"Ahhh... Whew."

Rika exhaled in front of the fifteen plates stacked up on the table as she poured another cup of tea. Chiho was even hungrier than before, but the story shocked her so much that she only managed five plates.

"Y'know, Chiho...?"

"Hmm?"

"Let's do it."

"Huh?"

"...Urp."

Rika took plate number sixteen out from the belt, already looking fairly pained as she brought a tuna-salad *gunkan* roll to her mouth.

"Um, you aren't pushing yourself too much, are you, Suzuki?"

"Yeh."

"Um?"

She was already on plate seventeen. It was no kind of meal a fit woman like her should be having.

"I gotta or I can't go on. C'mon, join me, Chiho. I'll pay."

"N-no, I couldn't."

"Please. There's no way I could ask Emi to do this."

One hand was on her lips while the other took plate eighteen.

"I really didn't get it. Even if Ashiya gave my feelings the nod and so on, I couldn't have really done anything. He's got his own future to pursue, and it's not the kind of future some girl on planet Earth he happened to run into can keep up with. But..."

"Suzuki..."

Plate eighteen remained on the table as Rika covered her face with her hands.

"But...it's weird. I've got no proof of this...but I can't help but think you can keep up with the future Maou's gunning for, Chiho. 'Cause right now...you've still got the freedom to choose your own future."

"Choose my future...?"

Chiho wasn't sure what Rika meant at first. Then it struck her, causing her to sit straight up.

"I mean, I may not look it, but, you know, there's a lot for me to shoulder and stuff, so..."

"Suzuki?!"

"I'm sorry. I tried my best, but now that I'm full, I'm kinda...letting my emotions go. This is really good..."

"Oh, don't cry, Suzuki. I mean, me too..."

"I'm older than you and stuff, too... I'm sorry. I get dumped in the most pathetic way, I turn to food to deal with it, and I'm sobbing my eyes out. I'm sorry."

"...!"

Chiho stood up from her facing seat and jumped over to Rika's side, hugging her by the shoulders.

"It's all right... It's all right."

"I'm sorry... I—I know this is just as hard for you, Chiho."

"It's fine. It's fine."

"Nn... Nnngh..."

Rika leaned into Chiho's shoulder a bit, gritting her teeth.

"If I had it my way...I'd rather he told me never to see him again... Then I could make a clean break finally..."

"...Ashiya's too kind for that."

"He's too kind, yeah... If he had to go that far, why'd he...? Why'd he have to worry so much about my—my health and stuff...?"

"It's totally something Ashiya would do. Really."

"I love him... I still love him now..."

Chiho kept hold of the quietly sobbing Rika until she calmed down.

By the time they split up, it was nearly eight o'clock. Rika apologized to her when they did, now fully composed again—but as she watched her go through the Sasazuka station turnstile, there was none of that nice, easygoing, big-sister type present, the lady who liked wheedling Chiho and Emi more than anything else.

"Suzuki..."

Kaori told her to stand strong and put her feelings straight across.

But that's just what Rika did, and it both literally buried her and did nothing to put her emotions in order. That scared her. She never thought about that when she made her own confession to Maou—but when the answer finally came, would it mean a final, decisive split away from him?

"What should I even do?"

What about Rika? With her mind still a mess, would she start avoiding Ashiya or the town of Sasazuka in general? It didn't feel that way to Chiho. Even if she and Ashiya didn't become an item, after that bold stand she made, wouldn't she still want to be near him? Or would being so close and never managing to cover that final gap crush her? She didn't know. No matter how much she thought about it.

"Huh? Chiho? Why are you out of the doors now?"

"Agh?!"

Right then, Chiho leaped at the voice erupting from behind her.

"A-Acieth?!"

Acieth Alla was standing there, chewing on a chocolate ice cream bar in the frigid night, carrying a shopping bag full of other snacks.

"Going home from the work or something?"

"N-no, just back from having dinner out..."

"Dinner?! Now?! Me, can I join?!"

Her willful ignorance of the words *back from* exasperated Chiho, but the realization that Acieth hadn't changed her ways one bit made her smile in relief.

"Sorry, but I'm full. Besides, if you go out to eat somewhere right now, that's gonna melt, Acieth."

Chiho pointed at the ice cream bar in her mouth. She nodded back, as if noticing it for the first time.

"Mmm, yes, maybe so..."

"Are you alone right now?"

She looked around. None of Acieth's more or less guardians were near.

"No, not alone."

"Oh?"

The obvious contradiction in her answer made Chiho freeze.

"I am going home from eating the dinner, but Amane and Erone, they became lost, so I search for them."

"Huh?!"

Realizing what had happened, Chiho wordlessly took out her phone and called the number Amane gave her for emergencies. She picked up on the first ring, a bit out of breath.

"Chiho! Hey, have you run into Acieth or anything?!"

"Sure have. I ran right into her at Sasazuka station… Sure, I'll wait here."

With a grin, she promised to keep Acieth in place until Amane could run over before hanging up.

"You see? It is why Maou should buy *me* the phone, too, when this happens."

"Ha-ha-ha…"

It was the perfect picture of brazenness from Acieth, whether she herself realized it or not.

"By the way, Chiho, were you with the other person? I can smell Rika a little from you."

Chiho stared at her. Acieth was right, but how could she have *smelled* that?

"Wow, I'm impressed you knew… Ah."

The surprise of it all loosened her lips a little too much. Chiho instantly regretted it. Acieth was currently shacking up at Shiba's house adjacent to the apartment, but she was a regular visitor to all the tenants inside. Emi would be there soon to pick up Alas Ramus—what if Acieth ran into her and told her Chiho was with Rika? That struck Chiho as something to avoid for now. Rika would probably tell Emi herself sometime, but until Emi had a better hold of herself, learning the news from Acieth would put far too much stress upon her.

"Oh, um, Acieth? If Yusa is at the apartment, can you keep it a secret that Suzuki was in Sasazuka?"

"Huh? Why?"

What could she say to make Acieth understand? It was easy for Chiho to picture her saying something like *Rika was together with Chiho, but it is secret, so I cannot say it!* to her. But there was no way she could tell

Acieth the whole story. Acieth wasn't deliberately bad, but she had no mute button at all.

After several moments of thought, Chiho built a story that would be safe for Acieth to blab about.

"Um, well, we got invited by Laila to see her place tomorrow."

"Mom's place? Ooh. Yes, there was the place for her, eh?"

Even a mystery archangel needed someplace to live in, after all.

"Right. And usually Suzuki's one to talk about her troubles with Yusa, but Yusa's got enough trouble dealing with Laila right now. So Suzuki came to me instead this time."

Acieth briskly nodded, still chomping away. "Ohhh. I wish Emi was more the, um, flexible with family."

"I'm totally sure Suzuki will talk to Yusa later on about it, so can you keep quiet about it for now?"

"Okay! Yes, it can't be helped! Secret is safe with me!"

"Ha-ha-ha... Thanks."

Chiho was less than confident about this, but there wasn't much more she could do.

"But still...Emi and Rika, they are same, yes? If there is something to say, just say it fast or else lots of regrets. I know there are the issues, but sometimes I see them and I really worry."

"Oh? What do you mean?"

"Mmm? Me and my big sister, we were separate for such the long time. So say the thing when you can, before you cannot say it anymore. Eat the thing you want when you can!"

"Before you can't say it anymore..."

The last part of it was a bit off-kilter, but the passing remark from Acieth held heavy meaning for Chiho.

"Acieth, have you...ever not been able to say it anymore?"

"A little."

Acieth stuck her thumb and pointer out, marking a distance in the air that meant nothing to Chiho.

"But now I see my sister and Erone again. Maybe I had chance and lost it, but you know, that was not last chance forever. But, you know, the wait until the next time, it was really rough."

"...Mmm, really?"

"Really, really! So, Chiho, say the thing you must say. Eat the thing you must eat! Okay! Here is one for you!"

"Um, thanks."

She was having trouble keeping up with Acieth's flow, but Chiho accepted the packet of gum planted in her hand anyway.

"Ooh! I haven't seen this in a while. They're still selling these?"

It was a cheap package with a picture of an orange on it and four balls of bubble gum inside.

"Mikitty said the balls, they are smaller than the past, but do you know, Chiho?"

There was a time in Chiho's youth when she was obsessed with the stuff. The first bubble gum she successfully cajoled her mother into buying for her was this exact type—a memory she never thought she'd recall here. That was the first of several occasions, each ending with her happily blowing bubbles as she skipped down the street. But then she lost interest, and she'd hardly tried the stuff since. She had liked it a lot, but now she couldn't guess when the last piece of orange gum she had was.

"I guess I've changed, too, while I wasn't paying attention."

Was that maturing or just changing? She didn't know. All she knew was that it took time to recall the things she adored as a kid when she ran into them again—those crushes that you unconsciously shunted into the past all the time.

"I don't want to make it a thing of the past."

"Mmm?"

Chiho smiled, grasping the small pack of gum. "Thanks, Acieth. I feel a little bit better now."

"Oh? I dunno what you are meaning, but you take more, if want. Eating always makes better!"

"Huh? Oh, I don't need that much!"

"No need for the politeness! This is not my own money, that I buy with!"

"That's all the more reason not to take it! …Ah, thank you, that's enough!"

Despite the Urushihara-style heinousness of Acieth's spending habits, Chiho wound up accepting three packets of gum, two boxes of caramels, and five different snack bars. All this was fished out of her shopping bag, so she must have paid money for them—likely provided by Shiba or Nord. No way Maou would ever trust her with cash.

As she thought about this, Chiho spotted Amane on the other side of the rail-station mall, Erone in tow.

"Chiho! Whew, thanks a lot! You were coming home from going out?!"

"Good evening, Amane. That's right. I was having dinner with a friend..."

"Ohh. Well, thanks for helping out. Come on, Acieth! I told you not to wander off like that! And where'd you get that ice cream and all that candy from?!"

"I think she bought it with the allowance someone gave her, maybe?"

"Someone too weak to defy her, I'll bet. Either Nord, Laila, or Aunt Mikitty!"

Chiho completely agreed. And considering the retro bubble-gum purchase, Shiba was likely the victim.

"I *cannot* believe this. And did you know that all-you-can-eat deals aren't all-you-can-eat, either? The manager can stop you anytime they want!"

"Um, neat..."

So after eating so much of the restaurant's pantry that the manager had to intervene, Acieth still had enough room in her stomach for ice cream and sugary snacks. It gave Chiho a fright to think of.

"I tell you," sighed Amane, "we should really start looking for places with those 'eat this massive sandwich, win money' deals! We'd clean up!"

Something told Chiho this wasn't a good idea. Given Acieth's knack for timing, she'd no doubt throw in the towel when she had one more chicken wing or whatever left to eat.

"But anyway, I'm taking you two back to the apartment! Thanks again, Chiho! I can't accompany you since I have *these* hellions to deal with, but take care on the way home!"

"See ya, Chiho!"

"Bye-bye!"

"See you. And thanks, Acieth!"

Chiho sighed a bit as she watched the two distant Sephirah relatives walk off. She felt bad for Amane, but as much fun as both of them seemed to be having, she could just barely imagine how much time it took for them to see each other again, laughing and smiling and saying what needed to be said to the other.

Even if her feelings didn't quite come across, she still wanted to see them through, rather than condemning them to the past. Merely waiting around, waxing nostalgic about it long after the fact, would be the worst thing she could do.

"Nothing ventured, nothing gained, huh?"

Rika really was a good big sister to her. When Chiho hemmed and hawed about taking action, Rika pushed herself into doing it. She didn't just unconsciously push those emotions into her past.

But she had a more pressing concern—namely, the double handfuls of candy she was now carrying.

"What should I do with this? I don't have my bag..."

"Chiho? What're you doing here?"

"Oh! Mom!"

Just then, Riho Sasaki walked out of the station and gave her daughter a dubious look.

"What's a good girl like you running around this time of night for? And all that candy, too?"

Her mother gave her a friendly grin as she took a caramel from Chiho.

"Wow, this sure is an old brand. As far as I can remember, I think these caramels were the first candy you harangued me into buying for you. I didn't realize they were still on sale."

"Huh? Really? I thought it was bubble gum."

"Oh, you begged me for all kinds of candy back then. Boy, were you a ravenous child!"

"Wow... Really?"

"Mm-hmm. So what did you do for dinner? Not just this candy, I hope."

"No, um, I had a friend invite me out to the conveyor-belt sushi place over that way."

"Ooh, look at that! A piece of candy used to satisfy my little girl, but now she's going out and eating at fancy sushi places! You must have a lot of free money, hmm? I'll be expecting something very nice next Mother's Day."

"Mmm? I guess so, yeah…"

Chiho gave an ambiguous smile as she dumped the candy into her mother's purse. They continued to chat aimlessly on the way home, both feeling more than a little relieved.

*

"Oh, Emi! Welcome back!"

"Acieth? What're you doing out this late?"

The sight of Acieth with a shopping bag in front of the apartment made Emi do a double take.

"I ate dinner with Amane and Erone, and at station, I run into Chiho and we talk!"

"Chiho? At this time of night?"

It was odd for Chiho to burn the midnight oil like that if she wasn't at work.

"Today, who is big sister together with?"

"Bell. Alciel said he had something to do out this afternoon, and the Devil King was at work, too."

"Oh! Can I visit Suzuno? I have the question to ask her."

"Hmm? You should be fine…but let's ask."

Acieth climbed the stairs behind Emi. The light was on in Room 201, Ashiya's and Urushihara's voices just barely audible. His date with Rika must be over, she surmised. A date that filled her with trepidation. But Alas Ramus came first.

"Hi, Bell! Hi, Alas Ramus!" Emi chimed.

"Emilia?"

"Mommy! Hiiii!"

Both voices made their way through the door, one after another.

"Can we come in, Bell? Acieth said she needed to ask you something."

“Hmm? What is it?” Suzuno asked as she opened the door, letting both of them in after seeing Acieth behind Emi.

“Oh, you work, too, Accith?”

“No, big sis. I bought snacks, a little early.”

“I wan’ some!”

“Whoa, Acieth, don’t show those to her. It’s too late to eat those.”

“Aww, tell me before now…”

“Now, now, Alas Ramus, we’ll save that for tomorrow.”

“Keh!”

Ever since she heard about Acieth and Erone plowing through five-thousand-yen worth of MgRonald combo sets, Emi had grown a measure pickier about Alas Ramus’s eating habits. There was the small but rigid thought in her mind that she couldn’t let her daughter be as gluttonous as these guys.

“Mommy is telling you this so you don’t get cavities, Alas Ramus. You need to be patient.”

“Aww, but Accith’s eating them!”

Suzuno’s lecture had little effect on Alas Ramus, now engaged in a rare pouting session. The sight of the little sister being allowed candy treats while the big sister was barred from them must have put her off. The speed of their respective growth presented certain unsolvable problems like this all the time, but there was no point explaining it to her in detail, so Emi simply put Alas Ramus in her lap and rocked her back and forth.

“So,” she asked Acieth, “what did you want to ask Bell?”

“Not just Suzuno. I want to ask you, too, Emi.”

“Oh? What about?”

“I heard you both go out tomorrow. You will?”

““Huhh?””

Emi and Suzuno both gave her odd stares.

“Go out where?”

“Huh? You are not going?”

“Going where?”

The conversation from the surprised-looking Acieth was going nowhere fast.

"You and Suzuno, you go to Mom's house, no? I heard."

"“Wha—?!”"

That exclamation represented both Emi's and Suzuno's surprise.

"If Emi and Suzuno go, then I know Maou go, too, and Ashiya and Lucifer, too?"

"Uh? W-wait a second! Who did you hear that from?!"

Acieth turned toward the frantic Emi. "Chiho said to me, she said, 'We go to Laila's place tomorrow'! So I thought you go, too, Emi!"

If Chiho were here, she'd no doubt be rolling on the floor and holding her ears by now. Acieth stuck to her word, mentioning nothing about Rika, but everything else was fair game. She couldn't be blamed for assuming "we" included Emi and Suzuno, given their cozy relationship, and the fact that Ashiya and Urushihara were enemies of Emi's was a tad beyond her comprehension. But Emi never told Chiho she was coming, or anyone else for that matter, so having word spread to the contrary wasn't exactly fair to her.

"We-we're not going."

"Uh? No? Suzuno, too?"

"Er, likely not, no. I had no intention, at least..."

Emi and Suzuno didn't have a clue how this topic came up between Chiho and Acieth in the first place, but neither of them had any intention of going near the place.

"Wait, so when Chiho says 'we,' she only means Maou and Ashiya and Lucifer?"

"If you are talking about tomorrow, I heard nothing about Alciel and Lucifer visiting, either."

"Huh?! So tomorrow, it is just Maou and Chiho and me?!"

Acieth was inserting herself into the equation for the simple fact that she couldn't be too physically separated from Maou.

"I think my father's going, too, but..."

"So Dad, Maou, Chiho, and me at Mom's place... I have the feeling the talking there will be awkward. Nothing to say!"

It was a surprise to see Acieth demonstrate that much care for someone besides herself, but she was right. It was hard to imagine what kind of conversation those members could even have with one another.

"...So, yeah, sorry, but we've got no plans to visit Laila tomorrow. If it gets too awkward, you can always go inside Maou's body, right?"

"Ooh, yes, but going on the long trip like this, you know..."

Just as Acieth was frowning at this—

"Goin' on a trip, Accith?"

The word *trip* triggered a flag in Alas Ramus's mind.

"Uh-huh! To Mom's place with Maou and Chiho."

"Daddy and Chi-Sis..."

"""Ugh."""

The impending signs of doom emanating from the child atop Emi's lap caused both her and Suzuno to tense.

"Mommy!"

"Um, what is it, Alas Ra—?"

"Field trip!!"

"F-field trip?" Emi parroted back, tone rising at her daughter's resolute face, voice, and hands gripped around her arm. "Y-yeah, uh, how about we go to the park by the rail line with Emeralda—"

"No!! Wif Daddy!!"

Emi's childish feint could never fool Alas Ramus.

"L-listen, Daddy has to go out on an important, um, job? We can't be a bother to him..."

"Why's Accith okay an' I'm not?!"

"Um, well, Acieth is more grown-up than you at the moment—"

"No! I'm big sis!!"

"Y-yes, I know, but..."

The candy refusal earlier had put the child into full rebel mode.

"Uh, it is not really the 'job,' yes?"

The added dagger from the absentminded Acieth was enough to put even Suzuno into a panic.

"Acieth! Emilia is not talking about that!"

"Suzunooo, no lieeees! Parents, they do things like that sometimes, but if you think the child is fooled by that, ooh, you think wrong!"

"Why do you only start making sense at times like *these*?!"

"Mommy...you lie?"

"A-A-A-Alas Ramus, I'm not. I'm not lying! Daddy's really out on a job, okay? It's just that—"

"Daddy 'n' Chi-Sis 'n' Mommy, all same job! Why don't you go, Mommy?!"

Describing it as a job was ill-advised. It gave Alas Ramus all the leeway she needed to hang on. She was being weirdly sharp and observant again, like how she was during battle sometimes, and Emi no longer knew if she could talk her way out of this.

"I mean, it's a different kind of job from normal."

"Accith said it's nodda job!!"

"Mm-hmm! Not a job! No sir!"

"Acieth! Please learn to read the room a little!"

"Yeahh, sorry, but if it's big sis, I take her side, okay?"

"Field triiiiip! Field triiiip wif Daddy!!"

"Whoa! Alas Ramus! It's late…"

"Nnnnnn-waaaahhhhhh! Fieeeeeeeellllldddd trrriiiiiiiiippp!!!!"

There was no bottling her up now. Alas Ramus was falling into a tantrum like none before.

"E-Emilia! Do something! I—I have never seen this before!"

"Me neither, Bell! P-please, Alas Ramus, just listen to me—"

"I wanna goooooooooooooooooo!!!!"

And amid it all, it was Acieth who picked up the howling Alas Ramus and rubbed against her, cheek to cheek.

"Aw, sis, so cute!"

"What the hell's going on in there?!"

"You're keeping the whole city awake, dude. What's up?"

"What is the meaning of this? I only pray that you have not done physical harm upon poor Alas Ramus!"

"Stay out of here, guys! You'll only make things worse!"

"*Wwwaaaaaaaaaahhhhhhhhhh!!*"

The sound of Maou, Urushihara, and Ashiya all storming out into the corridor and shouting through the door only agitated the child further. She jumped out of Acieth's arms and toddled toward the front door, Emi and Suzuno falling to their knees and pleading to the heavens above.

"Daaaaddddyyyyyy! Fieeeellllddd trrrriiiiiiiip!"

"Wh-what's going on? Emi, what'd you do to her to make her bawl that much? Open up, Suzuno! Don't worry, Alas Ramus! Daddy's right here!"

The concern was clear in Maou's voice as Alas Ramus batted her fists against the door, still crying.

"Here I am."

Acieth, the only person retaining any sense of calm, stepped up to unlock the door without the tenant's permission. Alas Ramus took the opportunity to bound right into Maou's arms, tears, snot, and all.

"Fiiieeeellldddd trriiiiiiip! Not just Acieth! Not faaaaiiiirrr!!"

"Huh? What's not fair?!"

Maou turned to Emi and Suzuno for some assistance. Both of them were still too dazed to offer any.

"Maou, you go to Mom's house tomorrow?"

"Um? You mean Laila's place?"

"Big sis, she wants to go, too."

"Oh? And that's what's making her scream at the top of her lungs?!"

"Fwweeeehhhhhh…snif…ngh…"

"All right, all right, calm down… Emi?"

"…………………………………………………………What?"

She held it in for ten seconds before half groaning out the one-word reply.

"Do I take this to mean you're not gonna go? Seriously?"

"……………………………………………………………No."

The news of her refusal never did get relayed to anyone besides Suzuno. Until now. Having it revealed like *this* was beyond her wildest nightmares.

"Man…" Maou winced, then took closer looks at both Alas Ramus and Emi. "You don't think *I don't wanna go* is gonna work with this girl now, do you?"

"…I can't just leave her with you or Chiho midway and go kill time somewhere else while you're gone?"

"Dumbass."

Emi's pointless struggling was effortlessly flicked away.

"Laila's meeting us at Shinjuku, but we have no idea where she's taking us after that. If we go too far away and she's thrown back into your body, how're you gonna explain that to her?"

"........................*Erg.*"

Emi groaned, still unwilling to accept defeat.

Even now, she honestly didn't want to know a thing about Laila. The more she knew about her, she feared, the more the assorted categories of anger she had for her might grow diluted, indistinct. Exactly like it had against Maou. Even if all that anger faded away, there was no way they could ever have a normal mother-daughter relationship.

The mere idea scared her. She had no idea how she should deal with Laila going forward, assuming she learned more about her. She had no idea how Maou and Chiho were going to settle the rift between each other. The weakness writhing in and around Emi's heart made itself known again—and it took Maou's calm rebuke to drive it away.

"Look, if you absolutely can't do it, I won't make you, but I don't think Alas Ramus is being so massively selfish here, either. If you can't win her over and it ends up with her like how it is with you and Laila right now, don't blame me."

"...!"

Alas Ramus almost never threw a fit like this. She was much more attentive usually, able to tell right from wrong. If she could tell that Emi didn't want to go, Emi couldn't deny that it might spawn feelings of mistrust between mother and child.

Her rejection of Laila was a backward-facing rejection, caused by her failure to face up to the simple confusion and indecision in her mind. Even she knew that Laila was slowly but surely making concessions, gaining a better grasp of what made her tick. That was why Emi had no firm motivation for refusing the request out of hand, and while Alas Ramus might not understand the details, she had a keen sense of her mother's indecision. *That* was why she wasn't listening to her.

"I think, um, time for the giving up?"

"……"

Acieth had to be doing all that on purpose. But Emi had no way of proving it. She looked up, resigned to her fate.

"Mommy…"

"Emi?"

Her eyes met the weepy face of Alas Ramus and the stern face of Maou. She drummed up as much energy as she could, ready to admit defeat.

"……………………………All right. I'll go."

THE DEVIL
AND THE HERO
FACE UP TO
REALITY

The western exit of Shinjuku station's Keio Line, the sight of dramatic events last night that were sadly witnessed by nobody on this planet, had a remarkable number of people hanging out by the turnstiles.

"Whoa! Acieth! No running around! Just sit tight like Erone!"

"Oh, come on, Amane! I can smell it! The curry! It is making me the very pulse pounding!"

"Curry spices don't work that way, man! Chill out or it's back *home* for you, Acieth!"

"And after all that rice she ate before we left… I tell you, Alciel was about to cry his eyes out."

"Are you feeling all right, Erone? You weren't scared of the train, were you?"

"No, I'm fine. Thanks, Nord."

"I would thiiink the traaain would be more scared of hiiim…"

"Keep it down, Emeralda! Erone's got a lot of hang-ups about that, okay?"

"Heavens be! Certainly are a lot of people in this station! Aren't there, Emilia? Hey, and I wish you could tell that kid to get used to me by now, mm-kay?"

"No thank you. If you want him to, try getting out of Alas Ramus's sight first!"

"Nnn. Why's Garriel here…?"

If they weren't all packed into a corner of the station, they would be a large enough crowd to block the flow of traffic during the evening rush hour right now.

Once all the bickering and carrying on subsided, the group assembled for the big tour of Laila's Japan residence began with original members Maou, Chiho, and Acieth, then expanded out to Emi, Alas Ramus, Suzuno, Nord, Erone, Amane, Emeralda, and special guest star Gabriel.

"Really, Amane, why *is* Gabriel here?"

The archangel certainly stuck out from the crowd—both in his social position and in his clothing. He had been Maou and Emi's nemesis for quite a while now, and even in this early winter day, he was still in his toga and T-shirt.

"Aww," Amane replied, "well, if Erone's goin' on the train, then we all know for a fact that if something happens, I ain't gonna be able to clean up the mess by myself, right? I think we *all* learned that the other day."

"...Would you like some curry, Erone? You, too, Acieth."

"Huh? Really, Dad?!"

"Are you sure?"

"Nord's spoiling them again..."

Picking up on Amane's discussion of the danger Erone posed, Nord decided to distract Erone himself with the stand-up curry restaurant right by the turnstiles, adding Acieth to the mix. Maou normally would've stopped them, but he could tell Nord was just trying to save Erone unneeded trauma, so he relented.

"So yeah, um, I'm here 'cause Ammie asked me to help, mm-kay? Mikitty gave me *very* careful instructions, so I promise I won't pull any funny business with all you guys."

"'Ammie'...?"

Whether Shiba was that much stronger than him or not, why was Gabriel acting so kind to the landlord and her niece, to the point of doing whatever they instructed him to do? It was a riddle to everyone in Villa Rosa Sasazuka.

"Yeah," Amane herself added. "And, y'know, they're all stable now, but there's no tellin' what kind of trigger might set Alas Ramus and

Acieth off. If worse comes to worst, I'd have to face three Sephirah solo, you see? If you were me, *you'd* want a little extra muscle, too."

"Sure thing, Ammie! Gevurah is one thing, but I'm kinda used to Yesod stuff by now, so— Though that pretty couple over there's sure givin' me the stink eye, so hopefully nothing happens, mm-kay?"

""*We're not a couple!!*"" Emi and Maou intoned.

"""...To the last millisecond,""" Chiho, Suzuno, and Emeralda all sighed in unison.

But Gabriel had a point. Emi had seen Alas Ramus go out of her control once, in the pursuit of Acieth. When fighting Camael's force in the Eastern Island, Maou could still remember how much Acieth's personality took on a violent streak. They both had to accept Amane's assessment.

"But stiiill, do you think we should let Erone and Acieth have curry right nowww? We meet with Laila at siiix, yes? Only five more minutes..."

"Nothing to be concerned about," Suzuno blithely replied. "I know Acieth is more than capable."

Chiho, for her part, pointed back at the restaurant. "See? They're already out."

"Wha—? That's rather faaast, isn't it?!"

It hadn't even been three minutes since Nord took the two Sephirah inside.

"Mmph. Yes, that will last the thirty or so minutes."

"Yum..."

"Urp..."

Compared to the completely nonchalant Acieth and Erone, Nord looked blue in the face and ready to hurl at any moment. Noting the horrified looks from the other diners rubbernecking at them from out the entranceway, Emi guessed at what just transpired.

"Must've tried keeping up with them. You all right, Father?"

"I—I think so...somehow. But I think I have discovered one of the grand truths of this world, Emilia."

"Oh?"

Nord glanced sideways at Acieth and Erone—Chiho currently wiping both of their mouths with a handkerchief.

"Curry is really a beverage after all, isn't it?"

"..."

She knew there was no point convincing him otherwise.

"So that's what chugging is, then? I thought it was discouraged as hazardous to your health, but..."

It was unclear exactly what her father was referring to. Emi wasn't sure she wanted to know. He was the one who should be yelling at them for eating that way.

"I better take better care of your diet, Alas Ramus, huh?"

"Oooh, only Accith again..."

Alas Ramus, in the newly resolute Emi's arms, gave a distressed frown once more when—

"Emilia?!"

Everyone on the scene turned around at the high-pitched voice.

"...........Laila."

Laila was standing there, a puffy jacket worn over her usual denim. She had both hands over her mouth, eyes glassy, a look of sheer shock on her face as she looked at Emi.

"You...showed up?"

"Not because I wanted to."

Emi readjusted her grip on Alas Ramus, keeping her distance. Her mother, she feared, looked ready to leap forward and embrace her.

"That's all right. I don't mind that. Thank you for making the time."

"......"

Laila was almost shedding tears of joy. Emi couldn't look her in the face, silently turning away instead. Not even for a moment did she want to see her mother happy. It might make her think, for the tiniest bit of time, that coming here was the right thing. Nord nodded deeply at this, even as he bit his tongue.

"And all of you, too... Thank you very much for taking the time to come here."

She wiped her eyes a little, then bowed her head deeply at Maou and everybody else behind Emi and Nord.

"Ah, you don't have to count me and Gabe. Aunt Mikitty just ordered us to serve as bodyguards, if it came to it."

"...Yeah." Erone solemnly nodded.

Laila took a moment to run a hand through Erone's black hair. "Really," she sadly stated, "there should have been a place for you to live your lives freely...but we took that from you."

"It's not only your fault, Laila," Erone quickly replied.

"Hey, uh, yeah, sorry about that and everything, but should we really be talking about that in the middle of this station?"

Compared to the crestfallen Laila, Gabriel sounded like he couldn't care less.

"Besides, apart from Erone, Acieth Alla, and this little kid, we're all on the same page in terms of what we know, right?"

"On the same page..." Chiho raised an eyebrow. "Are we?"

Was he talking about Laila's doomsday dossier? Chiho had taken a read through it, and Maou and Nord must have as well. Amane knew about Laila since long before, too. But Emi and Emeralda had been almost entirely hands-off with her, and—perhaps following her friends' lead—Suzuno hadn't had any particular relations, either. Ashiya and Urushihara, as potential negotiation partners for Maou, had to have heard the basics, but since Laila's plea was to save humanity on Ente Isla, a pair of demons like them couldn't have been terribly interested.

Besides, regarding Ashiya, Chiho had a concern that could barely be called a concern but still wasn't anything she could ignore. Was Maou aware of the fact that Ashiya hid enough demonic force to return to demon form before Rika's eyes? There was no way Ashiya could be attempting to overthrow Maou or anything—but it was hard to imagine him retaining that force without a solid reason.

Ashiya wasn't part of the group today—to keep the wholly uninterested Urushihara in check, as Chiho heard. But she couldn't believe that keeping an eye on Urushihara ranked higher in his mind than helping Maou come into closer contact with Laila. It seemed terribly out of place, like a piece of gristle in an otherwise fine piece of meat loaf, but discussing it with someone else could cause deep wounds to Rika's pride down the line.

Laila, picking up on her concerned expression, must have thought it was in response to Gabriel's question. She smiled a little at Chiho as she spoke to him.

"Enough of that topic for now," she firmly stated. "It is a violation of the terms Satan and I agreed on."

"Yeah, yeah."

Then she turned to the others. "Amane, I am unsure if Ms. Shiba told you or not, but my housing within the nation of Japan is located in the Nerima ward of Tokyo."

"Nerima?!"

"That's so nearby..."

"A decent distance from Mitaka," Nord felt it prudent to add.

"Wow," Maou added. "I've been put on support duty at Fushima-en over there all the time."

"You have?" a wide-eyed Laila asked.

The easiest way to reach Nerima from Shinjuku was to take the Toei Oedo Line in the direction of Hikarigaoka. Fushima-en, one of the most notable amusement parks within Tokyo city limits, was accessible by taking a branch of the Seibu Ikebukuro Line from Nerima proper. MgRonald had a franchise within Fushima-en, and with Kisaki's coworker and childhood friend Yuki Mizushima serving as manager over there, they sometimes traded personnel with each other.

"I've never been to Fushima-en, but I live in an apartment about five minutes' walking distance from Nerima Station. Ms. Shiba is my landlord, and she gave me a discount on the rent there. When I have work, I travel to Shinjuku from there."

"Work?" Chiho asked.

"Yes, I mean to explain that to you all today, too—what kind of life I'm leading in Japan."

"I see," she replied, before noticing something. "Wait, Laila, are you not feeling well?"

"Hunh?!"

Chiho's observation made Laila, for whatever reason, send forth a near scream of horror.

"Yeah," Amane rather rudely added, "you got these dark rings under your eyes."

"Oh, that, um..."

She made Laila lose her presence of mind for a moment, eyes turning to and fro before they settled on Nord.

"Listen, I know I said this before..."

"Oh?"

"But don't be too surprised, okay?"

"About *what*?"

"I tried. I tried really hard...but I've been so busy that I let things slide for far too long. There was only so much I could handle in one day's time."

What was she talking about? Nobody there had a clue.

"But—but anyway, let's get moving! Nobody has any objections to the Oedo Line?"

She tried her best to amplify her voice, despite her pallid complexion, as she took the lead.

"...What's with her?"

"I don't know."

Maou and Nord didn't know what to make of the bizarre tension Laila was letting off, but the whole group followed her anyway. Going through the Oedo Line turnstile to the right after passing through Keio Shopping Mall, they descended deeper down to the platform, barely in time to catch a train for Hikarigaoka. Compared to Tokyo's other rail lines, the rolling stock serving Oedo was a unique, more compact type. Acieth and Alas Ramus spotted it right off, and even Suzuno and Emeralda gave the trains furtive, curious looks, much to Maou's exasperation.

Laila sat down next to Nord, occasionally daring glances toward Emi, who would instinctively meet her gaze, then immediately avert it. This cycle repeated several times, forcing Emi to rather awkwardly turn toward Chiho each time. To Maou, well used to riding the Oedo Line and finding it not so rare of an experience, he felt painfully out of place.

Soon they were at Nerima Station. Back at street level, Laila once again took the lead as they walked the city blocks. They took a right past the turnstiles, winding up on a wide street that ran parallel with the train tracks, the Nerima Ward Office offering some eye candy to look at as they walked five minutes toward a residential neighborhood.

"...This is my apartment. On the third floor."

Laila had stopped at just another ten-floor apartment building in the area—walls of beige, no doubt housing a bunch of studios like every other structure on this street.

"Nothing very surprising so far," a wary Nord observed. "Compared to the apartment the Devil King Satan calls home, it hardly seems exceptional for an angel to be living here."

"It seems much less expensive than Lord Sariel's residence," replied Suzuno.

"I'd be surprised if it was," a smiling Chiho remarked. As the only regular human being in the group, she couldn't help but grin at this. After hanging around with Devil Kings and angels for so long, not even God himself living the next block over would shock her anymore.

"Pretty boring," came the final, damning appraisal from Acieth.

"It—it's pretty easy to live in, at least. The entrance is out behind the main street, so you don't hear much traffic. The government office and a lot of stores are right nearby, and so's the station..."

"Yeah, great," Maou moaned. "I'm still not believing you until we go inside."

"Oh...right..."

But here, of all times, Laila began to act all indecisive again.

"...This *is* your place, right?"

"It—it is. I really live here. Don't I, Amane?"

"Yeah, pretty much. It matches everything I've heard anyway. Why don'tcha look up there, Maou?"

"Mm?"

Amane motioned up at the gold-plated sign adorning the building.

"Royal Lily Garden Toyotama..."

Having a name like this for such a humdrum, nondescript apartment building was definitely a Miki Shiba touch.

"All right. Sorry. Need to rev myself up a little... Come on in. I think we can all fit in one elevator."

Laila headed into the lobby.

"...Hey, Chi?" Maou whispered toward the back of the crowd.

"Y-yes?" she replied, instinctively straightening her back a bit at the sudden voice.

"I'm sorry, but can you make sure you observe everything carefully here?"

"Observe... You mean in Laila's room?" she whispered back.

"Yeah. Like, whether Laila really lives here. Whether it really feels lived in to you."

"Lived in?"

"I mean," he said as he scrunched up his face, "whether it looks like a woman lives in there alone or not. I don't know what that should look like, so I might not notice if it looks all fancy on the outside. I want a female perspective. If you see anything that looks weird or unnatural, tell me, no matter how small it is."

"I—I dunno how much I can help with that, but... Oh!"

The elevator opened for them just as they made it inside.

"Um, sorry. Take the next one."

It filled up instantly, leaving only Maou and Chiho behind. There were twelve of them in all, counting Laila, a pretty tight fit for an elevator serving studio apartments. There might be larger elevators in bigger places for moving purposes, but it looked like this building had only one.

"We can take the stairs. Third floor, right?"

"Thanks! See you up there."

Gabriel jabbed at the DOOR CLOSE button the moment Maou stopped talking.

"...Sorry to put this on you," he muttered to Chiho as they stared at the closed door and heard the motor hum. "Like always, I've taken you too much for granted, and I knew that."

"Ah..."

Chiho gasped at this unexpected confession.

"You were willing to deal with it, so I always had you hang out with me, and I'm always making you tag along for stuff like this. I'm really sorry about it."

Just as, for example, she was assigned the stairs because she happened to be with Maou.

"I don't... I mean, I'm here because I want to be, so..."

"Yeah, but still, it's outrageous, the way I've used you without even trying to guess what was lurking behind your feelings. Ashiya really gave me an earful about it yesterday."

"Ah...?"

The unexpected introduction of Ashiya's name to the conversation made Chiho's heart skip a beat again. Why did he say something like that to him?

But Maou simply laughed instead of answering Chiho's curiosity. "Who knows when he was last *that* angry, huh? The day before that was pretty eventful, too, and even Urushihara is too afraid to butt in with his sass. Out of the frying pan into the fire, you know?"

She didn't know what those events were or what "*that* angry" meant. But if that was how Maou was putting it, she could easily imagine Ashiya reaching a level of rage that went beyond even what she personally witnessed.

"But...you know, Chi, you're so nice to me, I couldn't help but do it. Even now. I'm sorry."

His voice was halting—because he was at a loss for words, because he was choosing them carefully, or maybe because he still hadn't worked everything out in his mind.

"Man, I'm a wreck," he awkwardly continued. "I can't even put a sentence together. Um, if I'm being a burden on you, then just—"

"There's been a lot of times lately where I felt maybe I was being forgotten by you, Maou."

The word *burden* made Chiho open her mouth before she knew what was happening.

"But I told you a long time ago: I love you."

"Eahh?!"

The straightforward declaration made Maou yelp.

"I've never thought of you as a burden. You've always trusted in me, and that makes me so happy. If I could have the chance to spoil you, Maou, that's no problem to me."

She glared at the man, her lips tense.

"I'm still a young woman. I want to know why you put that trust in me or why you think I'm spoiling you. Just a little bit is fine. But I want to hear it from you, if I can."

"Uhhmm..."

The words that had reflexively come out of her mouth, Chiho realized, could be hiding the key to undoing the haziness in her heart.

"I don't doubt your trust or anything, and you aren't a burden at all to me. But really, I've never had any idea why you've placed so much trust in me."

She wasn't powerful like Emi or Suzuno. She didn't have any old bonds with him, like Ashiya or Urushihara. She hadn't saved his life, like Laila. She was just this new girl at work, and yet Maou was relying upon her for so much. Why? Trust between people, of course, is accumulated over lots of little events, often getting based on nothing more than vague impressions. That made it all clear how lacking Chiho was, socially, for all this trust heaped upon her.

"Could you tell me why sometime?"

But if such an answer existed, it would likely be the same thing as the other clear answer Chiho was waiting for. The answer to her question about Maou's own love. An answer that wasn't worth forcing out of him while people were waiting upstairs.

"...Honestly speaking, I really don't know myself..."

"If you don't, that's fine. But if you do figure it out, I want you to tell me first."

"...All right. I promise."

If Kaori were here, she'd probably chastise Chiho for giving Maou yet another reprieve. But this was about the best she could manage. A single choice made during his talks with Laila, and Maou might put himself into a deep, dark, potentially lethal situation. Asking him for this would be like trying to dissect his very psyche. It'd be nothing but stress, and Chiho didn't want to be a source of that for him.

"Let's go. Laila and everyone are waiting."

"...Yeah."

Guided by Chiho, Maou staggered his way over to the stairway toward the side of the lobby. The bewilderment clear in his behavior was heartrendingly painful to see, but the fact Maou had been seriously thinking about her made Chiho happy nonetheless. She grabbed his hand, pulling him forward.

"Hurry up or Yusa's gonna yell at you."

They hurried up the stairway, steps echoing upward, as Chiho felt the sensation of Maou's hand in hers. The dry winter air and his daily working habits made it feel cold, dried out, and a little rough. It reminded Chiho of the first time they had held hands. Back then, when the seedlings of yearning were building the foundation needed to bloom into true love, taking his hand required the most courageous decision she had made in her life up to then.

"Do you mind if we...uh, hold hands?"

"Sure, whatever."

The moment she felt a new sort of heat in her hand, she thought her heart was going to leap out of her throat. It was so surprising, so joyous, that she didn't even remember how Maou's hand felt. She was sure, though, that the way he reflexively clenched his hand around hers as she pulled it forward was exactly the same then as it was now. After everything she had gone through, she had no reason to doubt it.

"Not to put more pressure on you!"

"Huh?"

"But if I can be with you, Maou, I'd like to take the stairs slower than the elevator!"

"Wh-what's *that* mean?!"

"Exactly that!"

Maou seemed too confused to know what she meant by it. But that was fine for now. Chiho could feel the black morass that dominated her mind for the past few days finally go away.

"Did you have trouble finding the stairway?"

Laila was fidgeting on the third floor as she waited.

"Oh, we kind of lingered in the lobby a bit," Chiho said, bowing slightly before Maou could speak. "Sorry to keep you."

Laila didn't seem concerned. "No, I'm sorry you had to use the stairs. Anyway, that's my place over there. Room 306." She pointed at a door in a corner down the hallway. "I already told everyone else, but...try not to be too surprised, all right?"

Her continued warnings were starting to make even Chiho nervous. She tried to hone her perception like Maou asked, but her imagination couldn't help but go on flights of fancy. What if the door was connected to some kind of subspace, and she was sucked into another world the moment she opened it?

Taking a key out of her coat pocket, Laila inserted it in the door, took a deep breath, then turned back toward Nord, then Emi.

"I think this might be another trying…or, at least, embarrassing experience for you."

""Huh?""

"So I'm really sorry, all right?! This is my home in Japan!!"

Finally throwing all caution into the wind, she unlocked the dead bolt and threw the door open.

"Th-this…?!"

And the first exclamation of surprise came from none other than her husband, Nord.

⁂

"Oh, man…" Moau groaned with glossy eyes. "There's no way that wouldn't freak me out."

"It was certainly a shock," Chiho agreed. "I mean, something like that goes beyond sane living conditions…"

"Not even Lucifer would descend to that level," Suzuno added.

"Nooo, I am hardly in a position to criiiticize myself, but oh my worrrd…"

"I heard the two of them had squabbled in Emi's apartment," said Amane, "but this… Well, I hope Nord doesn't file for divorce."

"Mmm, yeah, they say irreconcilable lifestyle differences is one of the top reasons given for divorces, y'know?" Gabriel hummed.

"Yummmm!"

"I like this."

But even after that dreadful sight, Acieth and Erone still had the wherewithal to order yet another bucketload of food from the Mozz-Burger inside Nerima Station, leading Maou and Amane to question their sanity.

"Maou! The fries, they are more thick here than MgRonald's!"

"...Great."

"But the burgers are messier. I don't like them as much."

Seeing the Sephirah children express not a care for the world (or their blood sugar levels) made Maou feel overwhelmingly desperate for Alas Ramus's future.

Gabriel sipped on an Aserolla Hard Soda next to them. "So, Devil King? You more convinced about Laila now?"

"I sure wish I wasn't," the pallid Maou replied, shaking his head. He thought he wanted to know more about Laila's personal life, but he had no idea it was anything like *that*. Amane and Gabriel's chatter about divorce suddenly didn't seem like such a joke any longer.

⁂

"What...is this?"

Emi was the first to come up with a complete sentence.

"My goodness," Nord groaned again.

Laila remained there by the open door, looking apologetically toward the side. "...I'm sorry. I tried, but it was at such short notice, so..."

"Mommy, it's all dark!"

"For real...?"

"Whoaaa..."

"What on...?"

"Whaaa—?"

"...Pretty cramped."

"Um, are we safe in here?"

"What a mess."

The sounds of wonder and disgust filled the hallway, rounded out by Acieth exclaiming, "Ooh! Such the pigsty!"

It was, as she suggested, not even worthy of being called a home. Normally, it'd be a compact studio, maybe hitting two hundred square feet, with a kitchenette and unit bath attached. But as far as could be seen from the door, it was hard to tell where the kitchen ended and where the main living space began.

Around 40 percent of the floor space was occupied by books, 20 percent by clothing, and about 10 percent by cardboard boxes. The rest was merely piles and piles of…well, stuff, stacked up in the most disorderly fashion. Not stored—*stacked*. The door to the closet, normally used for clothes and bed linens, was taken completely off, a thick pole hung from it to the other end of the room. Dangling from it was such a grand variety of clothes that it formed a thick curtain blocking the view to the rest of the apartment. There were no bookshelves; instead, books of all shapes and sizes were haphazardly stacked everywhere, forming a sort of incline from the walls to the center of the room like an ant lion's pit. In the middle was a small heap of blankets, coiled around in a bird's nest–like clutch. Near the border toward what they assumed was the kitchenette was a low sitting desk like the one Urushihara used, a computer monitor perched on top of it that looked pretty vintage to Emi's eyes.

"This…is *after* you did your best to clean up…?"

"""Ah!"""

Her husband and daughter both gave her looks of disbelief.

"Um, well, when I'm not visiting your apartment in Sasazuka, it's usually because I'm pretty busy with work…"

"Work…? Hey, what do you do anyway?"

"Well…"

Laila reluctantly turned toward Chiho.

"Huh?"

"I'm actually a registered nurse. I pick up spot shifts instead of being assigned to a single place, but lately I've been settled down at the Seikai University Department of Medicine's clinic in Tokyo…"

"""""Whaaaaaaat?!"""""

The gathered shouts of Emi, Chiho, Suzuno, and Maou broke the silence.

"That's the hospital Chiho and Lucifer were kept in!"

"You—you're a registered nurse?!"

"No wonder you showed up in there!"

All three women were tremendously flustered. Not even Maou could hide his shock.

"Yo, Nord. Did you know that?"

"N-no, I heard she was in the medical field but not the exact location… Attaining a nurse's license isn't that simple a task, is it?"

"No. Not that I know the whole process, but you can't just get it in a year's time or anything."

Now nobody could hide their confusion. Laila's life seemed to be surrounded by layers and layers of surprise.

"I, um, I'm not lying. It's true. I made sure to frame my license and put it on the wall so it wouldn't get buried. Um, you might trip and fall if you aren't used to getting around, so let me grab it."

Were there trip wires installed in this room? What kind of place *was* this? Either way, Laila removed her shoes and went inside.

"Ow! Oh, um, I'm caught on something…"

They could hear her valiantly attempt to extricate herself. Then, after another pause, she came back with a picture frame.

"Here. See?"

She was right. It was a graduation certificate from a nursing institute, dated over ten years ago, certifying she had passed her qualification exam. And the name on it—

"'Laila Justina'… You kept your original name?"

Emi's eyes widened as she saw the name written out in katakana on the certificate.

"Y-yeah, I'm a naturalized citizen of Japan. I went to vocational school on a student visa first, and then I applied for citizenship after five years. Ms. Shiba's relatives helped out a lot with that. My records have me as being born in the UK."

Maou wondered if having her name out in the open like this exposed her to danger from her pursuers in heaven. But Laila was apparently resigned to that.

"I had thought about using a Japanese name, of course. But when I thought about how I could become a citizen and have the *humans* who live in this world recognize me by my name, that really made me want to use my real one. I wanted to think this was a world where people would accept me and the name I was given as a human."

Another piece of trivia that was picked up on by Emi, Suzuno, and Emeralda but no one else: Laila apparently wanted to have the last name she received from Nord be her official one in Japan.

"So now do you see how I'm officially established here?"

Emi wasn't sure how to respond to that. Her mother was far more committed to living here than even she was—although judging by this room, she wasn't exactly capable of going anywhere else.

"Oh, um, and if you want evidence that I'm working in a hospital, my next work assignment is in a couple days, so I'll make time if you want to visit!"

Laila must have taken Emi's apparent confusion as outright suspicion. She was all too eager to convince her daughter that she belonged here.

"All right? If you're worried, I can go find my residence certificate real quick. I think my electric and gas bills are somewhere nearby. Also...um..."

"...Any comment, Father?"

"Huh? Umm..."

Emi decided to address Nord, if only to remind her mother that she wasn't the only person in the room. He fiddled with his beard as he gingerly surveyed his wife.

"L-Laila?"

"Yes...?"

"Unless my memory is failing me...I don't recall you living in such squalor."

"I-I'm sorry! I, um, I'm on call at the hospital a lot, and there's all the Ente Isla stuff, and it's keeping me so busy that I'm hardly here at all unless I'm sleeping!"

Laila earnestly apologized at the expression of concern—or hopelessness—from Nord.

"Ummm," a voice called out, "I thiiink Laila isn't lying. It seems like her aboooode to me."

"Eme?"

Emeralda gingerly raised a hand. It notably brightened Laila, (incorrectly) assuming she was throwing her a life preserver.

"After Laiiila left, one of the dorrrm rooms in the Holy Magic Administraaative Institute was quite a bit like thiiis."

The life preserver turned out to be on fire, exploding in Laila's face. Her smile froze solid.

"Um—umm… I apologize for leaving it in that state…"

It was admirable of Laila to not make excuses for it. But she was no longer able to lift her head back up. The thought of her daughter's reaction scared her too much.

"While I was having Ms. Shiba help me establish myself here… seeing all these human beings living and thriving here, like nothing I'd seen before…it made me get a little carried away. Which I regret."

"In the middle of what's supposed to be a recession, too," Maou butted in. But Laila shook her head, expression serious if a bit covered in a cold sweat.

"I've seen too many countries where children who lose their parents are forced to finish their short lives begging on the streets. They say times are tough, but if a nation's full of people trying to make tomorrow better than today, that's what I call thriving. If everyone's looking in the right direction, the world's bound to reach a better place. That's such a happy thing to see."

"Yeah," her daughter said from beyond her eyesight, "but if you call this room of yours 'thriving,' then I'm not sure I agree with your interpretation of that."

"Oof."

"Lucifer's the exact same way. You angels are all such slobs. Now I'm a little worried about how Sariel and Gabriel are living."

"…I have nothing I can say."

"Yeah, I sure don't," Gabriel added for some reason.

"Uggh…"

Laila's body shrunk down at Emi's unseen sigh. But—

"…Yusa?"

Chiho noticed her face. It was surprisingly composed, vivid with color.

"If you've messed the place up this bad, do you think you're ever going to get your deposit back? Do you even know what living in an apartment means?"

"I think Aunt Mikitty will give it back to her as long as she didn't really mess up the walls and floor."

"That's not the issue, Amane. If you're living in a rented space, you've got an obligation to adhere to a bare minimum of cleanliness, at least."

"Oh, but wasn't there a Devil King who came to my shop because the room he rented had a gigantic hole blown in it?"

"That was *this* guy's fault, Amane."

Gabriel shot back at the spreading flames. "Hey! Not me! Your kid did that! This isn't the first time I've had these wild allegations against me, mm-kay?"

"What I mean is, even the Hero and Devil King need to clean their apartments once they go back home. I don't know what motives you have for lurking behind the scenes all this time, but I don't want to listen to someone who can't even keep her place decent."

"That..."

Laila's face was full of remorse, but given how obvious Emi's assessment was, it was difficult to take her side.

"...Hey, Emeralda, what're we gonna do about that? Emi's found another excuse not to listen to her."

"...Yeah, I wish she'd giiive up on it alreaaady..."

But it was also clear that Emi's indecisive attitude—a transformation in her personality brought on by her inability to decide on an approach to Laila—was starting to wear on her friends. Having lived in Emi's apartment all this time, Emeralda in particular had a front-row seat to this attitude of hers. Now they were all scared she'd use this dump as an excuse to turn on her heels and walk away.

But then Emi herself let off a bombshell.

"So I'm not going to listen to your story today...but I *am* going to clean this place up."

It instantly restored the color to Laila's cheeks.

"...Emilia?"

That offer was one thing. The mere act of Emi stepping inside and addressing her mother to her face was another.

"R-really?"

Emi took obvious pains to keep from locking eyes with her. "I just don't want my friends to think my own mother's living in a pit like this!"

"Emilia... Th-thank you... Thank you!"

In a roundabout way, Emi had acknowledged Laila as her mother. It made tears instantly well up in Laila's eyes.

"And let me just say, don't forget that you owe Eme, too. Trying to sponge off your daughter's friends... Could you get any more embarrassing?"

"I—I know..."

"And I can't believe you forced Father to take full care of Acieth even though you lived right near him. And don't tell me you weren't involved with Alas Ramus just getting tossed into Villa Rosa Sasazuka without a word. Do you have any idea how much pandemonium it was at first?"

"I know... I'm sorry."

"But..."

Here, finally, Emi softened her voice.

"I didn't imagine anything like this, but for the first time in my life, you're actually acting like you're alive to me. That's something, at least, I can take away from today."

"Yusa..."

"Emilia..."

"Oh, enough of that aaattitude, Emiiilia..."

Emeralda, along with Chiho and Suzuno, were all ever so slightly relieved to see Emi try to get a little closer to Laila, even with all the words she needed to get there.

"I could help you, Yusa..."

Emi turned Chiho down. "Thanks, but it'll be hard for too many people to navigate through all this. This is a family issue, and it's gonna take a family to fix it. And...sorry for everything, guys."

That short apology contained her fervent desire to atone for how weak willed she had acted for the past month or so. She rounded it out by addressing Maou, the man who had wanted to learn of Laila's lifestyle even more than Emi.

"What about you, Devil King? Seen enough yet?"

"...If you're happy, I'm happy. Go ahead and clean this place if you want. It's not like seeing this immediately changed my mind or anything."

"Ah. Well, thanks."

She informally raised a hand to see him off.

"...Hey. We're going."

"Whaa—?! We go now? Why did we come here?!"

Acieth had a point, but this peek into Laila's personal life was pretty much the beginning and end of Maou and crew's objectives. Acieth and Erone were brought along simply because their guardians couldn't leave them alone. But to Acieth, at least, she saw no point in going home yet.

"Huhh?! Come on! This is the total waste of time!"

"Ugh... Fine, you wanna eat somewhere?"

"That's the spirit, Maou!"

This carrot was the only way Maou really knew to keep her from whining until the cows come home.

"You just had some curry. Keep it light."

But now, he already sensed doom ahead as Acieth all but tied the bib around her neck right where she stood.

"We're headed home, Nord."

"Oh?"

The farewell left Nord uncharacteristically silent. Emi was already busy dissecting Laila's room behind him.

"Right! We're gonna throw away everything you aren't using any longer!"

"Wait, Emilia! I like those piglet-print socks! Those were the first ones I bought when I came here...!"

"No back talk! If they're that important, then wash them, fold 'em up, and put 'em away! Do you have any idea how neat the Devil King keeps his place? Have you no shame?!"

The cleanup battle between mother and daughter was off to a lively start.

"Do—do I have to stay?" Nord found himself asking.

"Of course you do. This is your wife and daughter here," Emeralda replied succinctly.

"N-no, I know that, but..."

"Have fun taking caaare of your faaamily!"

"No, Emeralda, umm..."

"Father, give me a hand! Go to the pharmacy and buy us some

dust masks! I'm gonna get asthma if I breathe everything in the air here!"

"See? Yusa's calling for you."

"Um, good luck..."

"I guess this'll be some good quality time for you guys."

"Yeah. Tell Laila that we'll hold down the fort on our end."

"Whoo-hoo! Time for the eating!"

"Hey, where should we go...?"

"Father! Buy some trash bags and twine and scissors, too!"

"Please, Emilia, wait! I'll wash these! And those are my textbooks! I still open those up sometimes! Don't throw them away!!"

As Nord blankly watched Maou and his cohorts file away from the apartment, screams and shouts began to erupt from inside.

"Honey, say something!"

"Don't spoil her any longer, Father!"

"...Granddad?"

Feeling something tugging at his pants leg, Nord looked down.

"Mommy an' her's kinda scary."

"They sure are."

Alas Ramus came to his aid, looking concerned. He lifted her up, a look of sorrowful resolve on his face.

"Better step up and help them out..."

"You think they'll make up?"

Chiho's eyes were watching far beyond the window.

"Who knows? They're closer to each other, at least, but I don't know if they'll go all the way."

"Well, if they're closooser, at least that presents more of an opportuuunity."

Compared to Maou, Emeralda was certainly far less pessimistic, if not wholly optimistic, about their chances.

"But how was she planning to make a whole bunch of angel feather pens in that mess?"

"Oh? Pens? What do you meeean?"

Surprised, Emeralda took one of those feather pens out from the shoulder bag she purchased in Japan. Chiho marveled at the dull glow.

"Whoa! I haven't seen one in real life before! It's pretty!"

The angel feather pen in Emeralda's possession was granted to her by Laila long ago, allowing her and Albert to travel to Earth in search of Emi.

"Yeah," Maou retorted, "and Laila claimed she could make one for all of us in that room if she wanted to. I dunno if she meant it as a reward or so we could all do something for her with them."

"...In thaaat room?" Emeralda frowned. "I don't know how they're maaade, but the end results would be rather dusssty, I imagine."

"No doubt. We know archangel feathers are used for them, but we don't know exactly how they're made at all. Hey, Gabriel? They didn't try writing with their own feathers long ago or something, did they? Like some kinda fairy tale?"

Gabriel gave this his usual cheese-eating grin.

"What if they did, hmmm?"

"If they did, it's kinda gross."

They may have been angels, but if you saw one on the street, they *looked* human, pretty much. A lot of wigs are made from real human hair, but that worked because they were processed in just the right way, used in the proper situations, so that it all worked without issue. The idea of angels plucking out their own feathers to make these pens was yet another blow to any sense of divinity they emanated in the demons' minds.

"Well, not that it matters if you know or not, but they aren't physically plucking out their feathers, mm-kay? There's a secret technique."

Gabriel's nonanswer made Chiho and Emeralda realize something at the same time.

"Ohhh? But..."

"Yeah. I heard the same thing."

They both looked at Maou.

"I think you told us, Devil Kiiing..."

"Demons aren't capable of using angel feather pens, right?"

Maou casually nodded. "Oh, yeah, I *did* say that, huh?"

These pens could only be harnessed by those in possession of holy force. Demons, who by definition don't have that, were blocked. A young Maou learned that from Laila himself way back when. But why didn't Maou react when Laila claimed she'd make a feather pen for him?

"I do not know how it applies with that feather pen, but if demons cannot use them, then what about Lucifer?" Suzuno asked from the side.

"It'd only half work, I guess? Maybe it'd make a Gate, but I wouldn't know how stable it was unless we tried."

"So...what about you, Maou?"

"Well, first, I figured maybe there was some special trick that'd let me use it. Second, the angels are still against us, so I thought we could glean some important info from them. That's it, pretty much."

"Ohhh, I see..."

"Some special trick, huh? I have my doubts."

Chiho thought about this a bit. Suzuno, on the other hand, continued giving Maou a concerned look.

"..." He shrugged, not indicating whether he noticed her or not. He continued, "Either way, Emeralda's right. No feather pen coming out of that hoarder's place is gonna work at all, and for all we know, she may be lying about the whole thing. Like, should a licensed caregiver really be living in such a mess?"

"I had no idea she was a nurse, though... Maybe she took care of me while I was unconscious in the hospital."

"Oh, she had to. There's only so many people who could've slipped that ring on you while you were sleeping, Chi."

"True."

Chiho recalled the ring with the Yesod fragment on it, still safe in its accessory case.

"'Course, it ain't so weird to think of Laila as a nurse at all. She used to work as a doctor long, long ago, so I'm sure studying for medical exams must've been a breeze for her, yeah?"

"Huh?"

"What?"

Maou's eyebrows shot up at the revelation Gabriel casually tossed into his reply. "Laila was a doctor?"

"Mm-hmm."

"Do they have...occupations, so to speak, in heaven?"

"They do, or they *did* kinda... But y'know, you can't expect everyone up there to be a first-class philosopher like Lucifer, mm-kay? Most of 'em are unemployed, and I'm not too sure any of 'em would work as hard as the salarymen of Japan. But hey, I'm employed. I'm guarding the Yesod, remember? Probably got fired long ago, for all I know, but..."

He smiled broadly to himself as he watched people go through the turnstiles to the Seibu Ikebukuro Line out the window.

"But back when Laila was a real doctor... Boy, that was back before we had become angels."

"Before you became angels?"

Suzuno and Emeralda gave each other concerned looks as Maou pouted.

"Ahh," a convinced-looking Amane replied, "that kind of thing? I couldn't get it out of your friend at Sentucky Fried Chicken, but when did you guys become angels?"

"Oh, you knew Sariel, Ammie? To put it in a Japanese kinda way, he used to sort of be a lawyer, by the way."

"What kind of crappy HR department do they have in heaven?"

Gabriel laughed off Maou's joke. "Well, we measure time on different scales up there so I can't give an exact figure, but... We've been angels for, what, maybe about ten thousand years?"

Ten thousand years. To a human being, who's extraordinarily blessed if they reach a hundred, it was a fearsome, incalculable amount of time.

"Gabriel?"

"Hmm? What's up, Chiho Sasaki?"

"Do you know why Laila's doing what she's doing?"

"Oh, more or less. We weren't in contact, so I don't know all the details...but I learned she was married right when you invaded Ente Isla, Devil King. Kinda indirectly once I learned about Emilia, but still..."

He must have known when the Yesod fragments were first deployed in Emi's holy sword and Cloth of the Dispeller.

"Now, unlike Laila, I'm more of a 'wait and see how things pan out' kinda guy, mm-kay? She decided to leave us, and I decided to stay put. That made for a pretty huge difference. Sometimes, we'd go for a century or so without talking to each other. But, like, it's the same for you guys, ain't it? If you go out with a friend for the first time in years, you start chattin' all day about the past, don'tcha? It's like that."

Maybe the situation was similar, but to a normal person, several months was quite a difference from several centuries.

"Can I ask a question out of curiosity?"

"Shoot."

"Laila wants Maou and Yusa to save the people of Ente Isla, right?"

"It wouldn't be totally right to say it's *just* that, but in the end, yeah."

"Um… How much time will that take?"

"Chi?"

Chiho's voice was serious, unshaken.

"Why d'you wanna know that?"

"When you kidnapped Yusa and Ashiya, all I could do was sit here and wait. I didn't want to join them, since I knew I'd be nothing more than dead weight, and Maou and Suzuno said they'd be back here as soon as they could. But it's not like a quest to rescue someone from another world normally takes only a week or so, the way it did with them."

"Hmm. Well, how much time do you think it'd take? You're one of the Devil King's ordained witnesses. I'm sure Laila told you at least some of the story."

"…She did." Chiho nodded, recalling the content of Laila's doomsday file. "And, um, if you asked me for a prediction, I'd say a month at the shortest, maybe even a hundred years or so at the longest."

"Wow!"

"Wh-wha—?!"

"A hundred yeeears?!"

"……"

Suzuno and Emeralda, unaware of the file and Laila's story, almost leaped out of their chairs. Gabriel lifted his eyebrows in fascination. Maou stayed silent, head down.

"Man. Chiho Sasaki. What a gal, huh? No wonder Laila counted so much on you, mm-kay? Can I ask," Gabriel said without denying the figures, "what made you come up with that time range?"

"You and Laila have been preparing for this for at least several centuries. People with your strengths and your life spans still needing that much time to work it out—it can't be anything too easy. But I also thought that maybe, as long as all the conditions were right, it's the kind of thing you can wrap up pretty fast once it's underway."

"Mmm. But that's not all of it, is it?"

"No." Chiho shook her head. "The Yesod fragment we call Alas Ramus is with Laila's daughter; Acieth is with the demon Maou. With everything positioned all crazy like that, the possibility of a really long-term mission seemed plausible, too."

"W-wait, Chiho. That doesn't make sense."

"How so, Suzuno?"

"Long-term or not, a hundred years? It is simply far too long. How would Emilia figure in that? It took her less than five years to defeat the Devil King, from start to finish."

"But this is different from beating the Devil King. I mean, Laila's basically asking Maou and Yusa..."

Chiho laid out the truth with barely a shred of emotion.

"...to defeat the almighty god of Ente Isla for her."

"""Wha...?!"""

Suzuno and Emeralda gasped.

"God, huh?" Amane listlessly asked as she stole a French fry from Acieth. "Of all the times for *that* to really show up. Talk about bad luck."

"Why would it come to that, Chi...?"

Maou attempted to halt Chiho in her tracks, before this idle chit-chat at the MozzBurger in Nerima Station became too apocalyptic, but it was Gabriel who stopped him instead.

"She was asking out of curiosity, mm-kay? You already know about all that, and the negotiations are strictly between you, Emilia, and Laila. But even they have the right to know the truth and think for themselves, yeah?" He vacuumed up the last of his soft drink and placed the cup on the table. "And they've got a right to turn to you for help, mm-kay? Even Crestia Bell and Emeralda Etuva. They're still Ente Islans, and they'll be rescued by all you guys, too."

"...Let me just say..."

He was right, but Maou didn't want to have Gabriel reminding him. On the other hand, he had nothing to counter with. So he merely gave Gabriel a goading stare before turning to Suzuno and Emeralda.

"You know," he warned, "I still haven't accepted any responsibility to do anything yet."

"Y-yes...but, Devil King, what will Alciel and Lucifer think of—?"

"Ashiya'll say to ignore it, what do you think? And Urushihara isn't sayin' anything at all."

"...Nothing?"

Maou meant to emphasize that his demon cohorts were acting perfectly normal about this. Suzuno wasn't about to fall for it.

"When will you finally face facts, Devil King? You are not lying, but you are not telling the truth, either."

"What?"

Suzuno frowned and stared at him. "If Lucifer really was against it, then he would say something like, 'Don't get me involved in this; it sounds like work and I want no part of it.' He wouldn't be silent. But he is, because he feels this is something he cannot afford to ignore, am I wrong?"

"......"

Maou looked suddenly daunted.

"I hate to agree with Gabriel, but I am still concerned about all of you, too. You could at least try to trust us a little."

"...Gahhh... I swear, what is with you people...?"

Maou brought a hand to his forehead, unable to look Suzuno directly in the eye.

"Maou," Chiho said, "I don't want to be separated from you and Yusa. I can put up with it for a year or so, like Gabriel said. But I can't wait a hundred. If you two were together for a hundred years, then I have to admit, that will make me pretty jealous."

"Oooh, Chiho! You go, girl!"

"But, I mean, I really love both of you, so..."

Chiho was all too receptive of Acieth's half-joking cheer.

"And not only me, either. There's Suzuno and Emeralda and the rest of the Ente Islans. There's Ms. Kisaki and Suzuki and Shimizu and Kawacchi and everyone else in Japan. There are tons of people who like you both. And none of them want to see their precious friends go somewhere far away for a hundred years. That's why I want to ask. Why did this thing you have to do wind up being something like that?"

"Didn't Laila tell you everything?"

"You know things that she doesn't, don't you, Gabriel? You told her that you'd take care of us for her."

"...This is just so hard to deal with, you know," Gabriel said, sounding like he was having much more fun than his complaint indicated.

"And Laila still hasn't compensated Maou and Yusa the way they need to be. She hasn't even made an offer yet."

"You mean about the metal? Or about having someone strong do something for her?"

Gabriel's strange analogy about Laila's compensation made Maou wince once again. The term *metal* reminded Suzuno of something for a moment, but Chiho spoke before she could fully recall it.

"I don't really understand what you mean, but I think it's probably the latter."

Her provoking eyes prodded Gabriel.

"And I haven't heard anything from you, Gabriel, or Laila, either, about how the Hatagaya MgRonald is going to plug the holes in the shift schedule if Maou and Yusa leave Japan."

Having someone who should be there just disappear—Chiho knew full well how heavy that really was.

"Holes in the schedule? Ha-ha-ha!"

It was Amane who laughed at Chiho's statement and the self-assured boldness she delivered it with.

"I like that kinda thing. Like, really."

Up to this point, she had been acting incredibly bored, ignoring the conversation and keeping a sharp eye on Erone. Now she was sitting up in her seat.

"In terms of where I stand on this, it's pretty close to Chiho. We're the ones having this huge job foisted upon us. If you ask me, the lives of individual people like Chiho and Rika over here are a lot more important than the lives of an entire race on some planet I hardly even know about."

"Amane..."

"I'm involved with the Sephirah, too, after all."

She smiled, her shiny teeth juxtaposed against her tanned skin, as she turned toward Gabriel.

"And don't think," she warned, "that Chiho's putting her fast-food job environment on the scales against the people of an entire world, okay? This girl's putting everything in her life up there, too, against what you want to rescue. That, plus the lives of Sadao Maou and Emi Yusa—two *people* that she knows and all the other people who know them. If you don't get how much that weighs, then even if Maou and Yusa say yes to you, Chiho's never gonna budge. She'd probably wage her life on trying to stop Maou. She'd want everyone in Ente Isla to die."

"Eesh. Well, I hope she doesn't do that. 'Cause if she pulls that when I have the Devil King and Emilia's agreement, well, that's gonna be an obstacle I'll try to rub outta the picture, mm-kay?"

"And then you'd be turning me and Aunt Mikitty against you. You realize what you're saying, don't you?"

"Yeah, yeah..."

As the archangel holding guard over the Sephirah, Gabriel knew or thought he knew the dangers of Miki Shiba and Amane more than anybody alive.

"All right. Lemme come clean, mm-kay? Maybe Laila ain't up for it, but there's somethin' I wanna have done so much, I'm willing to keep the Devil King and Emilia under lock and key for a hundred years, even more, if I have to. And I know this is gonna hurt Laila's bargaining position a ton with you guys, but me having Ashiya over for tea on the Eastern Island was related to that, although kinda distantly. But as for the reward for those hundred years spent, along with the potential for more that should've been earned along the way... Well, that we sadly don't have ready for you yet, mm-kay?"

"Well, rewaaards or not, a century is such a long tiiime... Even if she survived, Emilia would be an old woooman by thennn."

It was a matter-of-fact question. Gabriel gave it a matter-of-fact response.

"What, you think Emilia's gonna age and die like a regular human being? She's half angel!"

"Wait... What...?!"

Emeralda fell silent, as if someone had just punched her.

"How many years you think me and Laila and Sariel and Lucifer have lived and looked the exact same as we do now? Once we mature enough and our bodies reach peak condition, we angels stop. We stop getting older; we basically go on forever. If you fall from heaven, that's a different story, but Sariel proved long ago that Emilia's physically incapable of that."

Sariel had the power to banish angels from heaven, it was true. But when he opened his Evil Eye of the Fallen upon Emi, it stripped her of her holy force but did nothing to seize her ability to control the Better Half or transform into her half-angel form.

"You know that demons live for years and years, too, right? Not as long as angels, but still. And I don't know how many centuries this Devil King here's been living, but by demon realm standards, he's still in his prime. Probably hasn't even lived a tenth as long as me or Laila, mm-kay?"

"What's age matter once I'm mature enough, you?"

"Ever the young, ambitious upstart, hmm? Look, no matter how blessed with talent you are, you're still gonna be no better than anyone else when it comes to *experience*—those years you've built up. Young people get all pretentious, like *Ooh, you can't measure someone on age alone*, but what happens when they get older? Now *they're* the ones disparaging the younger generation, just for being there.

I've seen it all the time, mm-kay? But we're getting off track. If we go any further, it might be seen as me negotiating with the Devil King, so if we're gonna talk, let's keep it in the realm of chitchat with this li'l lady here, mm-kay? Or if you don't wanna hear it, you can always leave?"

"…Shut up."

Maou stood up, thoroughly annoyed, taking his wallet with him to the front bar. Being banished to an empty seat didn't exactly fill him with excitement.

"Right," Gabriel continued as he stormed off, "Chiho Sasaki talked about defeating the god of Ente Isla just now, but there isn't some kind of über-race higher up than us angels. It's just, y'know, kinda someone you could call our god, if you squinted enough. Someone who brought all us angels together, someone you guys might wanna defeat if you wanna save the people of Ente Isla. There are a lot of other bad hombres, too—Camael and Raguel, you know them—but compared to her, they're pocket lint, mm-kay?"

"…Her?"

Gabriel nodded at the question. Then he turned to Acieth and Erone, still scarfing down their meal next to Amane.

"Yeah, the boss of all us parasites. Slowly killin' the people who really need these kids."

He placed his elbows on the table, seeming to take delight out of Chiho's reaction.

"Before all that, she was a great leader, a scientist, a soldier, and a noble, merciful person. But then she extended her hand out someplace no person should ever dare reach, and it wound up pretty much wiping out an entire planet."

Emeralda spoke up at this, her knowledge of the universe still a tad hazy. "A plaaanet? Meaning a world besides Earth and Ente Islaaa?"

"You can put it that way." Gabriel nodded. "After that little tragedy, she's started doing this stuff that's really sinful, I know, but she mistakenly thinks is for the sake of the Ente Islans. Sadly, there aren't many people up there who think along the lines of me or Laila. I mean, Camael's her number one devotee, mm-kay? And that really screwed us over on the Eastern Island, actually."

He turned his eyes toward Maou, currently ordering some kind of dessert at the bar to the side.

"Now. There's someone me and Laila know, the person who originally proposed this whole plan we want the Devil King and Emilia in on. We're kinda taking on that person's mission, you know? And I'm not as serious about it as Laila is, since I'd like to kinda keep on living, but the more we've been observing Ente Isla, the clearer the data is that this guy was right the whole time. But she didn't understand that. So the two of them split off, and then war broke out. She won, and *he* was defeated."

Gabriel seemed to be basking in nostalgia.

"That guy—the guy who gave us the truth and ripped the heavens into two pieces—was named Satanael. Back when he was human, it was Satanael Noie."

"Satana…el?"

The name was repeated, then compared with the man whose back was turned to them near the register. There was someone with the name Satan in the heavens? Chiho had an idea who it could be—and she was quickly proven correct.

"That's the guy revered in the demon realm as Satan, the ancient Devil Overlord. He's also the cause, or the main perpetrator, of the Devil Overlord's subsequent Cataclysm."

Suzuno opened her eyes wide in surprise. Chiho gasped as well, recalling the old story Ashiya told her.

"He was human?"

"The Devil Overlord… The man who ruled the demon realm before Maou?"

"Yep." Gabriel smiled at the assorted gasps and eye blinks. "And the name of this god of ours, the one who killed the Devil Overlord, created the current heavens and rules over us…"

"God should never appear before the human race."

Even the rather strongly worded soliloquy of Amane was drowned out by the end of Gabriel's sentence—

"The name is this woman is Ignora, the mother of Lucifer."

– To be continued –

THE AUTHOR, THE AFTERWORD, AND YOU!

This afterword includes some spoilers. Please be warned if you are reading this ahead of the novel.

As I write *The Devil is a Part-Timer!*, I have taken pains to structure the story so you will have no problem keeping up if you've read the previous novels in the series, as published by Dengeki Bunko. However, one of the episodes in this volume includes a few references that may leave readers scratching their heads if they haven't read a short story published in *Dengeki Bunko Magazine* and not yet in the novel version.

Don't worry. There's a story behind that.

I've been reimporting a few characters and episodes from the anime version up to now, but generally I've introduced them in a way that'll make sense even if you're only familiar with the novels. However, quite a bit of Volume 13 of *The Devil Is a Part-Timer!* includes aspects that can't be fully told without knowing the episode in this short story, which involves the official history of the in-story world.

It's not that skipping this short story makes it impossible to understand the novels, but it will create a sort of information gap with people who didn't read *Dengeki Bunko Magazine*, which I feel really apologetic about. In place of that (if you can call it that, I dunno), I promise you that the short stories being published in *Dengeki Bunko Magazine* will make it to print in novel form sooner or later. For now, I appreciate your patience.

This afterword's getting a lot more businesslike than I usually go for.

Volume 13 takes a cornucopia of assorted smaller episodes and puts them all together to accelerate things along. Even so, time proceeds as normal, and all these people putting on clothes, working, eating, and sleeping at home every day are moving things along purely out of their own volition. Sadly, I, Wagahara, am not seeing my writing speed accelerate much to match, but here's hoping I will get to see all of you again as quickly as I can.

Until then!!